KATE'S BOOK

Mary Francis Shura

AN
APPLE
PAPERBACK

SCHOLASTIC INC.
New York Toronto London Auckland Sydney

ISBN 0-590-42381-9

12 11 10 9 8 7 6 5 4 3 2 1   9/8 0 1 2 3 4/9

Printed in the U.S.A.   11

First Scholastic printing, September 1989

Contents

1. February Snow, Ohio, 1843   1
2. Secrets   8
3. The Coming of Spring, March 1843   17
4. The Great Adventure   25
5. The Full May Moon and Tildy   39
6. Prairie Grasses   47
7. Harsh Words   55
8. The Gosling Drowneder   69
9. The Separate Ways   85
10. The Queen of the World   101
11. Flying Bears and Stars   113
12. Brown Water and Pink Roses   124
13. Old Bones, New Stones   136
14. The Thrashing   142
15. Wagon Fever   151
16. The Valley of the Bear   161
17. Silent Hours   172
18. Tears for Tildy   184
19. A Ring of Bright Stones   195

1
February Snow
Ohio, 1843

With her sixth-grade geography book open on her desk, Kate Alexander sneaked quick glances out the schoolhouse window.

The snow had begun falling during lunch. At two o'clock it showed no sign of stopping. Miss Jackson was drilling the little children in numbers. She didn't even seem aware that great flat flakes were splatting against the window and piling in drifts against the trees.

She *was* aware of Kate. "Kate Alexander," she called above the chanting of the seven-year-olds. "You will not find the map of Ethiopia outside that window." Naturally the other sixth-graders tittered. All except Jeb Haynes, of course, who snorted when he laughed. Maybe Kate's best friend Amy hadn't laughed, but Kate didn't dare look to see.

"Yes, ma'am," she said, forcing her eyes back to the page. She was her father's girl in all but this. He'd rather study maps than anything. She'd seen

1

him spend a whole winter evening pouring over a map as dull as this one. What could be more boring than a map, with nothing but lines that wandered every which way?

The little children were calling out their sevens when the sleigh bells sounded over their piping. Kate hugged her arms hard with hope. Miss Jackson prided herself on keeping proper hours. But if a parent came to get a child, he'd be excused. This could be Kate's brother Porter back from his trip to St. Louis, or even Papa himself coming to fetch her home.

"Seven times six," Miss Jackson prodded as boots scraped outside the door. After the briefest knock, the door swung open. Icy wind whipped around Kate's ankles, making a fan of snow across the floor.

"Begging your pardon, Miss," Kate's father said. Once inside, he had to lean with the whole of his weight to force the door shut against the wind. "This storm is rising. I came to get my girl."

He looked like a snowman with a frosting of white covering the whole of him. Kate felt smug and proud, looking at him. His face was rosy from cold above the fringed muffler she had knitted him with her own needles. As he pulled off his cap, his mass of unruly curls shone as bright as a copper kettle in that dull room.

Miss Jackson glanced at the window, her face

puckering into a frown. "The storm *could* be rising," she said. "Perhaps I should dismiss the classes early."

"Any who live along our road are welcome," he said, glancing at Amy and her brother Ned.

By the time they were bundled and out the door, other parents were arriving.

"You children hop up in the back," Kate's father said. "The front seat's taken."

"What's *that*?" Ned asked, staring at the massive, snow-covered figure who turned from the front seat of the sleigh to stare at them.

"It's a dog, lad," Kate's father laughed. "Haven't you ever seen a dog before?"

"Not like that one," Ned replied, squinching way back in his seat.

It was the ugliest dog Kate had ever seen, and the biggest. Under the covering of snow his hair was a wiry gray mat of curls. His legs were a mile long, but when he looked at her, he seemed to be smiling.

"It can't be ours," Kate said.

"Oh, but he can," her father said genially. "His name is Buddy."

"But what about Shep?" Kate asked.

"Is there a law in Ohio that a man can't have two dogs?" he laughed, smiling as he slapped the reins across the horses' backs and clucked them into motion.

3

"Could Kate come and play until suppertime?" Amy asked.

Kate's father shook his head. "That would mean a trip out later for your pa. Anyway, we expect Kate's brother to come riding in. I know she'll want to be there."

With Amy and Ned dropped off, Kate studied the dog again. "Why do we need a dog like that, Papa?"

"Guarding," he said, turning in at their own gate.

Kate caught her upper lip between her teeth. She decided not to ask what the dog would guard against. She hated being scared. If her father mentioned some new danger, she'd only have one more thing to worry about when she was supposed to be sleeping.

After a cup of hot tea and a wedge of cornbread with honey, Kate took her mother's sewing basket into the parlor. She knew that if she just went and sat down, her Aunt Agatha would be there in a minute, lecturing her about the evil of idle hands.

She hitched her sister Molly's red wooden stool close to the parlor window. Although the stool was just right for little Molly, who was only four, it was too short-legged for an eleven-year-old, like herself to use for anything but watching out of the windows. From here she could see her brother Porter the minute he turned into their gate. She desperately needed to talk to him. During the three weeks he had been off visiting their Uncle Whitmer Morrison

4

in St. Louis, all sorts of strange things had happened. This dog Buddy was only the last of the mysteries. Even if Porter didn't *know* what was going on, he'd have a guess.

Winter had etched the glass with a spidery tracing of frost. Leaning close, she blew a great breath of steam against the windowpane. Through this moist, clear circle she saw the unbroken white of the February snow still falling in great flat flakes. The yard shrubs were puffy mounds and the furrows of the plowed field beyond the fence as smooth as cream. With the trees of the windbreaks barren of leaves, she could even see her grandparents' house on the next farm over. Its wavering column of wood smoke rose lazily to be lost in the whiteness of the sky.

Sometimes she wished she had other relatives besides her mother's family, the Morrisons. Mostly she thought of this when her Aunt Agatha was prowling around being hateful to her. When she was younger, Kate had cried because her grandmother's sister clearly didn't like her, thinking she must have done something to cause this. By the time she was ten, she knew it wasn't her fault. Her Aunt Agatha just didn't like her looks, and nobody got to choose who they looked like! Kate, with her reddish gold curls and blue eyes, was the picture of her father, and no one in her mother's family (except her mother, of course) *really* liked Daniel Alexander.

That was all right. Kate loved her papa more to

make up for it. He was easy to love. He didn't stand as tall as a tree the way the Haynes men did, nor did he shout and bellow the way Amy's father did. Instead, he was strong and supple and always quietly smiling. Her Grandmother Morrison called him a dreamer and "fiddle-footed" because he was always hungering to see new places. He had come to Ohio in his teens, looking for adventure. Instead, he had found a wife and settled down to be a farmer.

But Kate knew he had only settled down on the outside. All her life, he had talked to her about the land beyond the Mississippi River. He called it the "Sundown Trail."

"Think of the glory of it, Kate," he told her. "To travel toward the sunset until you reached that shining sea." Every time a new caravan started west, his eyes turned wistful. He knew all about the equipment for the long trek, that a good wagon was expensive, costing between sixty and ninety dollars. A man had to watch the little details, he told her. The front wheels had to be small so the wagon could take sharp turns. The wagon bed itself had to be sealed well enough to float on water as if it were a boat. He knew the names of all the mountain men and was full of stories about them. The posters and handbills he kept by his favorite chair had big black letters across the top spelling out the names of the western territories — Montana, California, Oregon.

Kate blinked at the brightness of the late afternoon snow, wishing Porter would hurry up and come. She loved Porter almost as much as she did her papa. He had been her best friend all her life.

Maybe he could explain why her grandparents had started coming over almost every day when her father was away. They talked with her mother in urgent, angry whispers, but fell silent when Kate entered the room. Aunt Agatha, who usually came only to do extra sewing, had moved into the spare bedroom for a "visit." Her mother had acted vague and distracted, only half listening when Kate spoke to her. Her father was gone for whole days at a time, when he usually would have been tending his stock or clearing the fields for spring planting.

Now there was this dog.

And what could possibly be dangerous enough that they needed a guard dog as big as a yearling calf?

2
Secrets

Off in the kitchen Molly was chattering to her mother in the steady singsong that she kept up from the moment she wakened until she collapsed into sleep. Kate didn't realize her aunt had come into the room until she spoke.

"What are you up to there, Katherine?" her Aunt Agatha asked.

Kate turned, hoping her smile was convincing. She knew it was dreadful to dislike her grandmother's sister so much, but she earnestly did. Everything about her aunt irritated Kate. She was a heavy woman with a thin, pointed nose that was always red at the tip from either a winter or summer cold. Kate suspected she was bald because only the scantiest fringe of pale pink hair showed under the bonnet she never seemed to take off, even to sleep. She smelled of liniment and lye soap and, in spite of her size, crept around the house as stealthily as a prowling cat. If that weren't enough, her aunt was the only soul in the world who called Kate "Katherine," managing to pile every syllable of the name high with blame.

Since it was grievous not to honor your elders, Kate had never admitted her feelings about Aunt Agatha to anyone but her brother.

But Porter agreed that Kate had cause to dislike their aunt. Then, because he felt very grown-up at seventeen, he made a mild excuse for Aunt Agatha. "She probably acts that way because she has no proper business of her own," he reminded her.

Kate had giggled. "That's the same as admitting that she minds everyone else's business," she told him.

He laughed, his brown eyes dancing. "What a sharp tongue you have, Moppet," he said.

"I could have said lots sharper things," she told him. "I could have called her a busybody, a gossip — "

"Whoa," he cautioned her. "If the walls had ears, you'd have bed without supper tonight."

"I asked what you were doing," her Aunt Agatha repeated in a cold, aggrieved tone.

"I'm threading needles for mother's sewing basket, ma'am," Kate told her, adding the ma'am to make peace.

Her aunt sniffed. "It's a wonder that even such a clever child as *you* can thread needles looking out

9

the window. Best you tend to your work. You'll see more than enough of the outdoors before this is through."

When she swished from the room, Kate stared after her. Before *what* was through? What in the world did *that* mean? Could it possibly be related to the other strange things? But even if there had been no mystery, Aunt Agatha liked making veiled, threatening hints to keep Kate's mind boiling.

When she turned back to the window, Porter's mare Bridie was prancing up the drive. Kate thrust the empty needle into her mother's pincushion and slid from the stool. She caught her shawl from the hook inside the door and let herself out quietly to keep her aunt from noticing and calling her back.

The storm had stopped, and a slender curve of moon glistened on the snow as she started toward the barn. She ran swiftly to keep the drifting snow out of her light slippers. At the barn lot, she climbed through the fence and beat Porter into the barn. In the darkness she saw the gleaming eyes of the pumpkin-colored cat who fought an uneven war against the barn rats. He stared balefully at her from a cross beam, then shot off into the darkness when Porter led Bridie in.

Porter frowned with concentration as he lit the lantern. For a moment the harsh smell of kerosene overwhelmed the warm, rank smell of the hay and animals. How handsome Porter was in the sudden flare of light, and how much she had missed him! Kate's curly hair frizzled and coiled under the brush, but Porter's was a straight, glistening black like her mother's, and his eyes a deep chestnut color. His new mustache, which she still wasn't used to, glistened in the light and his teeth shone as he grinned at her.

"You're like to freeze," he told her.

Gripping her shawl, she stretched to hand him the curry brush. "I missed you. Why did you have to go, anyway?"

"I'm back now," he told her. "Never fret what's too late to change." He brushed Bridie without meeting her eyes. "Anyway, you knew I went to see Uncle," he reminded her.

"But you're not sick," she said. Her mother's brother was a doctor whom Kate seldom saw except when he was called home to heal a family member.

"Would I be likely to travel in bitter winter if I were sick?" he asked.

"No," she agreed in a mumble. "Porter, what's going on? Everything is strange since Christmas and no one will tell me why."

"Have you asked?"

She nodded. "I asked Papa why we needed that great new dog he brought home today. He said it was to guard us."

When Porter only nodded, she went on. "Papa

comes back after being gone whole days at a time. Then he doesn't talk about who he saw or what cattle he bought or anything."

What good was it to have a brother who was your best friend when he only listened silently and ran the brush in smooth, sweeping strokes across Bridie's flinching hide? "And Aunt Agatha has moved into the guest room as if she means to stay there forever."

Porter laughed and placed a fresh blanket across Bridie's back. "Now don't tell me she hasn't said why she is here."

Kate sucked in her breath angrily. "She doesn't tell, she only complains." Kate mimicked her aunt's resentful shake of the head and piped, "When a body comes to help out, one would think she could have a second cup of tea."

"You are a bad one, Kate Alexander," Porter said, leaning against the stanchion to laugh. "It's a cruel talent to be able to mock another person that well."

She glared at him. If she had wanted a lecture, she could have stayed in the house. She had saved the worst worry until last and hadn't meant to say it at all, but it just popped out of her mouth.

"Grandma and Mother both cry a lot when they don't think anyone is looking."

Porter stood very still a moment, then turned to her. Even through her shawl, his hands were warm on her arms. He lifted her and set her on the edge of the oat bin, eye level with him. All the laughter was gone from his face, which looked suddenly spooky from the shadows cast by the wavering lantern.

"You're too clever for your own sake by half, Kate," he said, his tone thoughtful. "There's a great decision being made in this family, and it's not one with a right and wrong to it. Once the decision is made, they'll be as open as spring with you."

"I want to know *now*," she told him. "If it's about the family, I should know, too."

He shook his head. "It's their decision and they'll tell you in their own good time."

"I'll explode," she told him. "I'll just blow up like a cow who's eaten green hay."

He stared at her and hugged her. "You crazy moppet! You'll not blow up, and you'll not die of curiosity. You'll be a good patient girl and accept what comes with good grace."

"How come you know and I don't?"

"Because I'm a grown-up and you're a child, and because I wouldn't go paddling down the road and tell Amy Lyons and Martha Vigners and the rest of that herd of little girl friends our family's business before it is time."

"I can keep secrets," she protested.

"Then prove it," he challenged her, swinging her

13

down to the barn floor with a thump. "Keep your eyes and ears open all you can but your mouth shut. Is that clear?"

"I hate it when Mother cries," she called, running after him.

He caught her arm and kept her in step with him. "And I hate it when you act like your Aunt Agatha."

She gasped. "How can you say an awful thing like that?"

"Whose business are you minding?" he asked.

Only a few days later Kate's friend Amy Lyons turned eleven. Kate was invited for cake and afternoon games in Amy's honor. More fresh snow blew in during the night. Porter hitched Bridie to the sled. Snow spangled in the sunlit air and the sleigh bells danced merrily all the way to Amy's house. Cuddled under the buffalo robe, Kate studied Porter's profile. How serious he looked, staring off into the snow. Now that his mustache was all the way in, he was working on a beard. It was only a shadowy darkness along the line of his jaw and chin, but it already made him look older. "You don't smile nearly as much as you used to," she told him.

He turned to her and grinned. "What do I have to smile about? I wasn't invited to Amy's party."

Kate giggled, "Don't be silly, you'd hate it. All those little girls! They'll sound like a dozen Mollys all chattering at once."

He laughed and tightened Bridie's reins, skating the sleigh to a stop, the runners squeaking on the freshly packed snow. Then he was at her side, lifting her down. Before letting Kate go, he hugged her tightly a moment. "I'm going to miss you, Moppet," he said.

"Aren't you coming back for me?" she asked, confused.

His face was suddenly a brighter red than even the windblown snow usually made it, and he patted her shoulder. "I don't know what made me say that. Of course I am. Have a wonderful time and give my best to 'old' Amy."

Kate could hardly contain herself until Amy opened the gift that Porter had helped her pick out. He agreed that a girl could hardly get a more grown-up and fashionable gift. When Amy saw the tiny scissors in their case, she squealed with delight. "Kate," she cried. "Thank you so very much. I will wear them forever to remember you by."

Kate frowned. To remember her by? When she picked out the scissors, she had thought of the fun she and Amy would have when they did their embroidery stitches together. Amy had a half-finished sampler and Kate was on her second one. She stared at Amy, who was suddenly too busy to look up. She had taken off the red cord that she wore around her neck and was fastening the scissor case to it. When she was through, she slipped the case in under her belt and patted it with satisfaction.

"There," she said, smiling at Kate. "I feel so fashionable that I can't stand it."

She *looked* fashionable, too. Her calico dress was sprigged with tiny red flowers, and her pantalets were of the same goods. Her slippers, which had little wooden heels, were tied with fringed ribbons.

The cake was made with white flour and must have had a whole day's gathering of eggs in it to make it so feathery and light. Mrs. Lyons, her round face flushed with pleasure, stood with the milk pitcher in her hands, and nodded at their compliments. Kate felt Amy's mother watching her before she spoke.

"So what is the news at the Alexander house?" she asked Kate brightly.

Kate looked up, startled. She swallowed hard to rid her mouth of cake. "Not much, I guess," she admitted. "Porter got home from visiting Uncle Whitmer last week and Aunt Agatha is staying with us."

Amy's mother waited a moment as if she expected more. Then, recovering herself, she began to fill the milk glasses around the table. Kate glanced at Amy and found her staring with wide, thoughtful eyes. Whatever had come over everyone that they acted so strangely?

3
The Coming of Spring
March 1843

The snow left gradually, melting from underneath to leave a glistening shell that wouldn't hold Kate's weight. Rivulets of clear water dripped and sang through the barnyard and cut an angled path across her father's field.

The mysteries deepened but Porter was still no help. In fact, he became one of the mysteries himself. He barely ever stayed at home. When he *was* there, he stayed in his room reading the thick black books he had brought home from St. Louis. He and her father spoke to each other as if they were strangers. Everyone had changed except Molly, who still wakened every morning talking, and went on chattering all day without ever even catching a breath. If no one was around, Molly talked to her wooden doll, Annabelle. If the doll was not there, she talked to the furniture.

The school year seemed to be lasting forever. Kate was bored with it, and tired of the cold walk to the schoolhouse and back every day. Even so, she told herself she was glad to go to school if it got her away from home.

Once there, however, the children she didn't really like got on her nerves worse than ever. She had always just ignored Jeb Haynes, who was bigger than she was and smelled bad. Suddenly the way he leered at her across the room and bumped against her when they walked through a door inflamed her with anger.

Even Amy, who had been Kate's best friend always, asked Martha Vigners to play jacks with her at lunchtime in Kate's place.

"You're grumpy," Amy told her. "I want to have fun, not be grumped at."

One afternoon Kate let herself in through the front door to find Molly plumped in the middle of the hall, talking away to her doll in her endless happy prattle.

"For heavens' sakes, Molly," Kate snapped at her. "Don't you know *how* to close your mouth?"

Molly stared at her with wide dark eyes and shut her lips tightly for a moment. Then she leaped up and ran wailing toward the kitchen.

"I heard that," Kate's Aunt Agatha said. "There's a cruel streak in you, Katherine Alexander, shouting at that poor baby who's the only voice of joy left in this house."

Kate started to deny shouting, then caught herself. Wouldn't her Aunt Agatha like that? Then Kate would be in trouble for impudence and "talking

18

back." She looked at her Aunt Agatha straight on and said, "Yes, ma'am," as sweetly as she could manage.

"Jane," her Aunt Agatha called with a note of desperation in her voice. "Katherine is being impudent to me again."

Kate's mother came to the door with Molly sobbing and gripping her about the knees. How tired she looked. Kate hadn't imagined that her mother had been secretly crying. Only shedding tears would leave such gray smudges of shadows under her mother's eyes. Her lips were pale from the pressure with which she held them together. Kate knew from her tone that her mother was struggling to keep her voice steady.

"What did Kate say to you, Aunt Agatha?" she asked without even glancing at Kate.

"It wasn't *what* she said, it was her attitude," the older woman told her. "She's completely out of hand, that girl. How can you even think of being able to handle her — "

"Aunt Agatha," Kate's mother's voice rose; half question, half rebuke. Whatever her aunt had meant to say stopped in her throat at Kate's mother's tone.

Her aunt made a little hissing noise, turned, and mounted the stairs to her room. Kate looked after her in amazement. The same shoes that she wore as she crept silently around the house made loud clattering noises as she stamped up the stairs.

"Come, Kate," her mother said. She shifted Molly to her left knee and drew Kate against her shoulder, holding her tight with her right arm. Without even meaning to, Kate began to cry. These weren't just everyday tears, but deep painful sobs that she couldn't stop once they started. "There, there," her mother murmured. "There, there, Kate." Kate waited for her mother to ask what was wrong, but she didn't. Instead, after a minute, her mother's tone brightened. "Splash a little cold water on your face and come help me. The water's at a boil and there are turnips to peel."

"I want to know why she is here," Kate said, not caring that it was a rude question.

Her mother looked at her very directly. "Your aunt is here because my mother's sister is always welcome in my house and she kindly offered to help."

Kate tightened her lips. "I can't see that she's doing anything except picking on me."

Her mother leaned over and selected a knife from the wooden board above the table. "Your aunt has done a great deal of sewing that needed doing. She's kept me and Molly company with your father and Porter away. In fact, Kate, it's a wonder she has energy enough left over to make such a martyr of you." She handed Kate the knife without smiling.

Kate flushed at her mother's sarcasm and bent to the basin of turnips. They were a glossy, almost waxy white with a brushing of lavender around their stem ends. They never tasted nearly as good as they looked, and they smelled awful, but Kate was glad to have her hands busy. Why had her mother said, "There, there" so tenderly if she were going to turn right around and pick on Kate herself?

But when Kate thought of it, grumpy old Aunt Agatha was right. Molly's was the only joyful voice around the house. Her mother cried, her father was either gone or buried in thought, and Porter now hid behind his beard, reading the big heavy books he had brought home from Uncle Whitmer's.

But what had Aunt Agatha meant about handling her? Putting it that way made Kate sound like an untrained colt who had to be broken to the rope and saddle. Kate had behaved well enough until her aunt came, didn't she know that?

As the blanket of snow gradually melted, one object after another became visible: the fence posts, the pasture watering trough, an abandoned cart.

In the same fashion, as the weeks passed, Kate became aware of more and more strange things that had either never happened before or that she hadn't noticed.

Her mother had clearly had some sort of a "falling out" with her parents. Her Grandmother and Grandfather Morrison stopped coming over at all, even though they had only a pasture and a field to cross to get there.

Strange men came and walked the fields with her father. They looked into the barns and stables while her mother watched silently from the kitchen window. Her father came home with great wooden boxes, which he stored in the back of the barn. When Kate asked him what was in the boxes, his tone was vague, "Oh, tools and such."

The worst of all was that Porter and her father quit talking to each other at all, even during dinner. And her father quit teasing her and Molly, as if he had forgotten how much he liked them. She remembered what Porter had said about her parents' "decision" and that they would tell it to her in their time. That time never came.

School went from difficult to impossible. Jeb Haynes never let a day go by without picking on her. He caught her in the schoolhouse entrance and slammed the heavy wooden door shut on her. Her bruised shoulder hurt so much she couldn't sleep. He tripped her at tag in the schoolyard, sending her sprawling into the mud puddle that gathered by the well.

Finally she had had enough. He jerked off her bonnet on the way outside to lunch. She swung her bucket at him angrily, not caring where or how hard she hit him.

She gasped to realize that the bucket had struck him square in the face.

By the time Miss Jackson got there, Jeb was

jumping up and down, howling and spraying blood all over the schoolyard. The teacher yelped in horror and began to mop at Jeb's nose with her smock. She didn't even seem to care about Kate. Her face went all pale as if she were afraid. Kate didn't blame her. Jeb had a great many brothers who were all bigger than anybody and smelled even worse than Jeb. They took pride in being known as fighters. Miss Jackson was probably scared of what they would do to her for letting Kate beat up on their baby brother.

"Kate Alexander," Miss Jackson cried when she finally caught her breath. "I can't believe you'd do such a thing. This is Ohio, not the wild West. Maybe you can get away with this kind of behavior out in Oregon, but — " She stopped with her hand in front of her mouth. Her eyes were wide. "Oh, my dear," she said. "I didn't mean to say that."

Kate, her curls tumbling all around her face from how roughly Jeb had pulled her bonnet off, stared at her dumbly. It was as if the inside of her head had been turned into a huge blackboard slate with immense words written on it:

WILD WEST
OREGON

At the same moment, everything made sense for the first time. Her father, who had always hungered to go westering, had finally made the decision. The strangers had come to look at the farm to buy it. Her father had been off those long days making arrangements. The boxes in the back of the barn were full of the awful list of supplies that the travelers always had to take with them. And her grandparents? They'd never liked her father anyway. Now they were mad past speaking that he was taking their daughter and her children off into the wilderness.

She stared at the teacher a long moment. Then, without a word, she walked over to Jeb Haynes, grabbed her bonnet out of his hand, picked up her lunch pail, and started down the road toward home.

"Come back here, Kate Alexander," Miss Jackson called after her. "It's only noon. You haven't been dismissed."

Kate didn't even *look* back. Jeb still lay on the icy ground, moaning. He recovered enough to yell after her, "I hope you get scalped."

The thought would have made her shiver except that he said it in a lisp, the way Molly had talked before her front teeth came in.

4
The Great Adventure

Her mother looked up as Kate walked in. Molly, on the floor trying to force a squirming kitten into a calico doll's dress, fell silent as she stared at Kate.

"Home already?" her mother asked with a confused glance at the clock. "At this hour?"

Kate slammed her lunch bucket down. "Are we going to Oregon?" she asked quickly before she lost her courage.

Her Aunt Agatha loomed suddenly in the door, watching and listening.

Kate's mother glanced at her aunt and hesitated.

"Why don't you come right out and tell her?" Kate's aunt said. "Everybody in this county has figured out what that fiddle-footed husband of yours is up to. *She's* going to be put through it, she might as well know."

Kate's mother's face flushed a deep, painful red. "Please, Aunt Agatha," she said, her voice trembling. "If you don't mind, I'd like to talk to Kate alone."

"I *do* mind," the older woman said. "Oh, don't worry, I'll leave the two of you alone. But I want it known that I do mind seeing you and that man drag these helpless little children away from their family and friends and the safety of civilization. The trail to Oregon is marked by the bones of innocent women and children."

Kate's mother waited silently.

"I'm going, I'm going," the older woman said. "But mark my words. You'll rue the day."

Molly had lost interest and resumed her attempt to stuff the protesting kitten into the dress. The room was suddenly full of sound, the ticking of the clock, the hiss of steam from the blue-spotted tea-kettle, and the helpless mewing of the kitten. In spite of this, a kind of silence hung between Kate and her mother.

"Come and sit down," her mother finally said, moving to the bench beside the polished pine table. She took both of Kate's hands in her own. Her hands were warm and felt moist around Kate's cold fingers.

"You know how much your papa has always wanted to go west?" her mother asked quietly.

At Kate's nod, she went on. "It's not right that a man give up all his dreams for his family. The Oregon Territory isn't just a wilderness anymore. Other people have settled out there. There's a great ocean and beautiful mountains and land to be had for the asking."

"He has land *here*," Kate blurted out. "And this house and our friends." Jeb's words must have struck deeper than she realized for she heard herself add, "And no Indians."

"The child's afraid," her Aunt Agatha said from the door. "And well she might be. Tell her she doesn't have to go. Tell her she's welcome to stay here where she's safe, with plenty of good food to eat and no privation. It's only fair to tell her."

Kate felt her mother's hands trembling. Then she pulled them away and stood up. "Aunt Agatha," she said, her usually calm voice vibrating with anger. "I asked you to leave me alone with my daughter. Now I ask that you go back to your sister's house. I can't have you interfering with my family's business."

" 'Your sister's house,' " the woman repeated. "That's your own mother you're talking about. This isn't your family. It's *our* family you're tearing asunder on this wild, reckless adventure."

"Go back and read your Bible again," Kate's mother told her. "My place is with my husband, and I cleave to him."

This time Aunt Agatha really left. Banging sounds came from her bedroom overhead, and Kate's mother sighed, turning Kate's hand in her own. After a moment she spoke. "I can't believe I was so rude to that poor, lonely old woman." She paused, and then rose. "Help Molly get her wraps on, and your own. We'll take Aunt Agatha home in the buggy."

Kate felt scared. If only her papa were home to go with them. Instead, Kate led out Chessie and held the bridle while her mother hitched up the buggy. Together, she and her mother bumped her aunt's brass-bound trunk down the front stairs.

All that time Aunt Agatha was as bad as Molly. She never shut her mouth, but kept saying over and over, "To think I'd live to see the day I'd be sent packing from my own niece's house for just telling the truth." She sniffed a lot. "Don't bother about me," she protested. "I can just walk across the fields in the mud and slush and have my things dragged over somehow."

Kate's mother said nothing. With Kate's help, she loaded the trunk in the back of the buggy, then offered her arm to help her aunt up.

When she reached her parents' house, instead of rapping at the door and going right on in, Kate's mother used the brass knocker and waited like a stranger at the front door.

Kate's grandma and grandpa answered the door together, standing side by side. Kate had never noticed how much of a size they were, almost like twins. They both had white hair, and were thick around the middle, and wore glasses. Neither of them smiled. Kate's stomach began to boil and tumble as if she had eaten live snakes for lunch.

"Don't stand in the cold," her grandfather said, stepping back. "Come in."

He led them to the parlor instead of the warm sitting room just off the kitchen. When her mother perched on the edge of the rosewood chair, Kate sat down, too. Molly took a stool by the hearth and stared at all of them with brown saucer eyes.

"Kate's teacher told her today that we were moving to Oregon," Kate's mother said. She wet her lips with her tongue before she went on. "Aunt Agatha and I had some words about the trip and I asked her to come back here."

Kate didn't have to look at her grandmother to know how she would feel about *that*.

"I thought it was only fair to give you a chance to talk to Molly and Kate about it."

The clock in her grandparents' hall had a slower, heavier tick than the one in the kitchen at home. It seemed to mark a lot of moments before anyone finally spoke.

"Katherine," her grandmother said. "Look up at me."

Kate did, but her heart was thundering and when she said, "Yes, ma'am," her voice wavered.

Her grandmother's tone was wonderfully gentle. She didn't say anything ugly about Kate's father, nor threaten Kate with privations the way Aunt Agatha had. She only talked about how Kate could stay in her school, and with her friends, and how much she and Grandpa loved her.

"This big house has plenty of room for you and Molly to grow up in just like your mother did." She stopped suddenly, as if her voice had been pinched off.

"Later, if things work out for your parents in Oregon, you could go to see them. Maybe you'll even want to settle there yourself when you're all grown up."

Kate looked at her mother in astonishment. Why didn't her mother say something? How could she just sit there primly with her hands tight in her lap? "Mother," Kate wailed. "I don't understand what this means."

"It should be plain, Kate," her mother said without even a tremor in her voice. "Grandma and Grandpa want to keep you children here when your father and I leave for Oregon."

Kate stared at her. "Stay with Grandma and Grandpa? But we're *your* children."

"You're also their grandchildren," her mother said, "and the only ones they have. It's natural they don't want you to go."

Kate began shaking her head. Her body trembled with the shock of how calmly her mother was taking all this. Didn't she even love them anymore? Could she really just walk away like this? What about Papa? He wouldn't let them be taken away from him, she knew he wouldn't.

"Mama," Kate wailed again without meaning to. "You can't mean you'd let them take us away. Don't you want Molly and me? Don't you even love us anymore? It's not natural at all. We belong with you and Papa."

When her mother stood up, her face looked strange and flushed. Her mother didn't look at her but spoke firmly. "That's enough, Kate," she said. "We'll talk about this later. But I think it's settled now." She nodded at her parents and reached for Molly's hand. "Thank you for letting us come." Her voice sounded curiously formal as if she were bidding farewell to strangers.

As Kate's mother led Molly and herself out of the door and into the buggy, a torrent of angry words followed them. "You'll all rue this day," Aunt Agatha wailed. "It's madness, real madness." Both of Kate's grandparents' voices rose and fell in anger against the background of Aunt Agatha's shrill fury.

Once in the buggy, Kate's mother sat limply for a long moment.

Kate, her hands tight in her lap, blinked back the hot tears that had gathered behind her eyes and looked straight ahead. It would never be the same again. No matter what happened, she would always remember that her mother would have let her go with only a few words.

Finally her mother spoke quietly. "I guess I can't expect you to understand, Kate," she said, her voice heavy with despair. "Your father and I felt you deserved the chance to make your own choice."

When Kate didn't answer, her mother reached over and lifted a coppery curl from Kate's forehead and looked into her eyes. "You can't know how hard it was for us to put you through that scene. And we were *very* sorry you had to hear about our plans from outside. We tried to keep it private until we were sure we could go. It's a long trip, Kate, six months or more. And it takes a lot of money to prepare. We only knew for sure we could do it when Papa found a man to buy the farm. Kate, can you try to think of this as a grand adventure?"

"I can try," Kate said. After what had happened, how could she keep on talking about the trip? What good would it do to tell her mother that the trip didn't seem very important at all? Even though she wished her aunt and Jeb hadn't used such scary words as privation and being scalped, the trip had somehow shrunk in her mind. Would they have left her, gone off and left her there forever if she had simply said the wrong words? Even with the buffalo robe tight around her shoulders, she felt cold.

* * *

With her Aunt Agatha gone, Kate did feel more cheerful. She never mentioned the scene at the Morrisons to her father. Deep inside she was afraid to learn that he would have let her and Molly stay. Even if that were true, she didn't want to know it. Instead, she clung to him, spending every minute with him that she could, reminding herself that no matter how her mother felt, her papa loved her and would never go away and leave her.

With her father's arm around her, she studied the map he spread out on the kitchen table. "We need to get off as soon as we can to meet our wagon train in Missouri," he told her. "And this is the path we will follow."

The trail wandered north and west like a lazy worm in no haste to find an apple. The rivers were black squiggles with their names printed in and the mountains little haystacks lined up one after the other. Beyond the last mountains lay a slender strip of land and then the peaked ruffles of the ocean with a ship drawn on it in full sail.

"There," he said, pressing his finger on that little piece of land. "*That* will be our new home."

After that the time passed swiftly. Kate's parents talked of nothing but the coming trip. Her father, having the choice of traveling to Missouri by river or starting out in his wagon from home, had chosen the latter.

"That way I'll *know* the wagon is made as it need be," he said. "It'll also give me time to get used to the new beasts before we hit the trail."

"The beasts" turned out to be four pale oxen. Kate, who had only seen oxen from a distance, watched her father lead them into the barnyard.

"What are their names?" she asked.

Her father turned to smile at her. "Now *there's* a question. How about you name them for me?"

Kate climbed over the fence and stood looking at the animals thoughtfully. How huge they were, with thick bulging shoulders and sharp cloven hooves. They might have been scary with their great curled horns except that their expressions were wonderfully gentle. They seemed as interested in her as she was in them. A fly droned by and tried to crawl into the first ox's dark, flaring nostril. He whipped it away with his great rough tongue without taking his big expressive eyes from her face.

"Touch one," her father urged her.

Kate put her hand on the ox's shoulder. Its flesh was warm and smooth under her hand. He rippled his muscles under her touch and looked back at her.

"Oh, I do like them, Papa," she said, in a rush of feeling.

"They are noble beasts," her father said, nodding. "Blessed with patience and gentleness and great strength."

"Do we know four noble names?" Kate asked.

"One could be King, another Prince." She hesitated.

"Duke," her father suggested. "Then there are earls."

Kate giggled. "Like Earl Jamison in my class? Wouldn't he laugh to know I named a great beast after him?"

"*Would* he laugh?" her father asked.

She nodded. "Earl is ever so good-natured. He's as big as Jeb Haynes without being mean and stupid the way Jeb is."

"Then I would say our beasts have been named."

Things happened so swiftly that only a few sharp scenes stood out for Kate. The March moon rose full, with a luminous ring around it as if it were lit by a lamp from behind. Kate stared at that strange moon from her bedroom window. Could this be some kind of omen? She couldn't ask anyone, especially not her mother. Her mother frowned at talk of superstition and was apt to give Kate a lecture on being "afraid of her own shadow."

But while "the great adventure" sounded splendid, the little pieces inside it terrified her: the rivers, the mountains, and Indians. Porter went off to St. Louis again. When he didn't come home, Kate remembered that St. Louis was in Missouri. She decided that Porter and Bridie would join them when they got to the meeting place in Missouri. Most of their furniture went back to the Morrison house since it belonged to Kate's mother's family. A week before the date set for departure, Kate's father carried a wooden chest up to her room. "Pack carefully," he told her with a smile. "There'll be no shopping for a good long time."

She packed and unpacked the chest until she cried. The problem was the list her mother gave her. Oilskins and boots and all those cotton dresses used up her space. Finally, by mashing everything way down, she fitted in some things she really wanted: her horn-backed mirror with the matching comb, her needlework, one sketch book, and some pencils. Kate gave everything that was left over to her friends or to the charity barrel at church.

Amy gave a farewell party for her. Although they played the games they'd always played, nobody seemed to have a lot of fun. The hard part was the way they looked at her. She wanted to cry out, "It's me. I'm Kate." But still they stared as if she were a stranger.

Kate's aunt didn't come back to visit once. Neither had Kate seen either of her grandparents again. How could they love her enough to want to keep her, and not enough even to say good-bye?

They planned to start at dawn on Monday morning. That Sunday night when they left to call on the Morrisons, her father whistled Shep up into the back of the buggy beside Kate.

When Kate looped her arm around Shep's neck, he panted happily in her face. "Look who's going visiting," she told the dog.

Her father spoke quietly from the front seat. "Shep is moving in with the Morrisons, Kate," he told her. "He's too old a dog to make that long trip. It's better that he stay with the fields he knows."

"He'll come running after us," Kate warned, tightening her grip around the dog's shaggy neck.

"Your grandfather's hired hand will keep him penned until we are too far for him to follow."

Kate fell silent, fighting tears. If she had agreed to stay with the Morrisons, her papa would have left her, too, the way he was leaving poor old Shep, who had been her friend forever.

"He'll be all right," her father told her.

Didn't he know that "all right" wasn't enough? She might have looked all right, too, if they had left her, but inside her heart would have been broken into smithereens.

"He's been my dog all my life," she finally wailed.

"That is why he is too old to go westering," her mother said quietly. "Eleven is young for a girl but very old for a dog like Shep." Kate clung to Shep and fought back tears as her father turned in at her grandparents' driveway.

How odd it was to be received like strangers! Kate's grandmother shook her hand and passed her cookies. Molly leaned against her grandfather's knee and chattered into his face. He nodded now and then but never touched her. The conversation rose and fell with little silences between. Kate's father glanced at the clock, and they all rose.

"We wish you Godspeed on your journey," Kate's grandfather said coldly. Her grandmother snuffled quietly into her handkerchief.

Before they even reached the buggy, Kate's mother began to cry. Kate's father braced her with his arm as Kate and Molly straggled along behind.

"They will never forgive me," Kate's mother wailed. "Never in this life."

"Nor will I forgive them," her father said. "Remember, they are keeping our son."

Kate stumbled in the dark road, feeling something rough and painful press against the back of her throat. "Papa," she cried. "What do you mean? Where's Porter?"

He turned and took her hand. "Listen to me carefully, Kate, because I will never speak of this again. Your brother has chosen not to go west with us. He plans to be a doctor and is studying with his Uncle Whitmer in St. Louis. You may claim to have a brother if you will, but I no longer have a son."

The stars spun in the darkness. If she had chosen to stay with her grandparents, would he have denied he even had her as a daughter, too?

5
The Full May Moon
and Tildy

The numbness that started with Kate's father's words didn't go away. Porter couldn't be gone. Kate's hazy ideas about the trip to Oregon — the herds of buffalo, the shining mountains — all of these had all been bound up with Porter riding along on Bridie, Porter to talk to, to laugh with. She couldn't imagine life without Porter because he had always been there, like her mother and her father and the wide fields stretching off toward her grand-parents' house. Molly didn't count because she had come later. But Porter had always been there.

They left before dawn. Fog wove like ribbons in among the trees and smelled green, like spring. A cock crowed as they passed the Morrison farmhouse, its windows still dark from the night.

Kate's mother drove the oxen. Her face was flushed from fear of the great beasts, but the only other sign was a tightness in her lips and her silence. Noble they might be and gentle, but the oxen plod-ded along with exasperating slowness. Kate's father rode his mare, Chessie. With the help of the great dog Buddy, he herded the rest of the livestock along behind the wagon.

Kate had never been so tired in her entire life. By nightfall the numbness had become a heaviness, and she ached all over. She was tired of the eternal bumping of the wagon, of Molly's singsong voice, and of thinking about Porter. Neither had she ever been so sad. Her tiredness and sadness churned together to become a lump of anger in her chest.

"Porter didn't even tell me good-bye," Kate told her mother.

"He didn't rightly have a chance to," her mother reminded her. "He was hoping to get back before we left but he didn't make it."

"He wasn't *whisked* off to St. Louis," Kate said. "He went of his own accord. He could even have stopped by my school on his way out of town. He was only thinking about himself."

Her mother's brown eyes turned thoughtfully to her. "Porter has a right to his own life, just as your papa does, and you do."

"I didn't choose to be bumped along in a wagon all day," Kate told her.

"I believe you did, Kate. You could still be back there on your grandmother's painted porch."

When neither of them said anything for a long time, her mother spoke up again. "Maybe you'd feel better if you got out and walked a while. Shall I ask your father if I can slow down to let you off?"

Kate shook her head. "I'll just jump."

The nice thing about walking was that Buddy galloped up at once to romp along beside her. She found a stick and threw it. He ran so fast that he scooted right past it. He braked on all four legs, turned, and came bounding back with the stick, his feet thundering on the hard earth.

At nightfall they stopped. For the first few days they ate cooked food that Kate's mother had carried from home. After that they made supper over a fire whose embers still winked scarlet when Kate crawled into the tent to sleep.

The states *felt* a lot bigger than they looked on the map. The days bumped along like a bad dream that wasn't ever going to end.

"It'll be different when we join up with the rest of the train," Kate's father told her. "You wait and see."

All the way from Ohio, Kate's father had talked about meeting the train at Elm Grove in Missouri. Kate imagined great green trees in a wide meadow. When the sun was low in the western sky, they joined a flowing stream of wagons pouring into a crowded noisy space with two lonely trees, a large one and a small.

Even after dusk settled in, the emigrants kept arriving, filling the plain with more horsemen and cattle and wagons. Tents of every description bloomed everywhere and the air grew rich with the smell of meat sizzling over dozens of campfires. A full moon silvered the tops of the wagons as Kate squatted near their fire listening to the camp music. The fiddles and banjos all played different tunes. Each time Kate picked out one to hum along with, it was drowned out by a louder strain. When Buddy, at Kate's side, growled deep in his throat, Kate looked around.

The girl had come from behind the shadow of the wagon to stand staring at her. She looked to be about Kate's age. Her bonnet shaded her face, and its strings hung loose over her dark checked dress.

"Is that dog mean?" she asked, nodding toward Buddy.

"I don't think so," Kate said. The girl's voice startled her. It was deep and a little gravelly for a girl and not the friendliest she'd ever heard. But Kate wasn't used to strangers, having gone to school and church with the same children all her life. She thought maybe she should say something friendly, but no words came.

The girl squatted beside her, eyeing Buddy suspiciously. Closer up, Kate could see that she was round-faced with a short upper lip and a little snub of a nose that made her look younger than her age.

"I've seen smaller ponies in my day," the girl said. She turned to Kate, her eyes curious and bold.

"Where you from?"

"Ohio," Kate said.

The girl leaned, fished a half-burned stick from the fire, and began to scrub the sparks from it in the dirt. When she glanced up again, she looked cross. "All right," she said. "I'll give you one more chance. What's your name?"

Kate stared at her. "My name's Katherine." She blinked. Why in the world had she said that? "That's my whole name," she added swiftly. "Everybody calls me Kate."

"That's better," the girl said with satisfaction. She sat on the ground, folding her legs tailor fashion under her skirt. "I'm Tildy Thompson. That's short for Matilda, which is about as bad as Katherine."

"What did you mean, one more chance?" Kate asked her.

Tildy shrugged. "One person can't do *all* the talking. We're supposed to take turns. I say something, then you say something. Otherwise it's not fair."

Kate laughed. "I have a sister who's happy to do all the talking," she said.

"A sister!" Tildy said, staring at her. "Are you ever lucky! All I have is big, mean, dirty, smelly brothers." As she spoke, she slammed the stick hard on the dirt, sending up a spray of bright sparks.

Kate stared at her, suddenly envious. It had been splendid enough just having *one* brother. "How

43

many brothers do you have?" she asked.

"Dozens," Tildy said, her tone almost a growl. "Dozens and dozens and dozens."

"That's ridiculous," Kate said, not even caring if it made the girl mad. "Nobody has dozens and dozens of brothers."

Without warning, Tildy laughed. It was such an unexpected and astonishing sound that Kate stared at her. Tildy's broad, warm smile showed her front teeth with a little gap between them. "That's how it *seems*," she said. Then, as if she didn't even mind being caught in such an outrageous fib, she asked, "What kind of a dog is that, anyway?"

"Papa says he's a wolfhound."

Tildy's mouth dropped open and she stared, first at Kate and then at Buddy. "He'll *really* come in handy. The wolves are something fierce where we're going."

Kate said nothing, not having heard anything about wolves.

"See?" Tildy said crossly. "There you go again, not doing your part of the talking. You need to meet my brother Sam. The cat's got his tongue, too. What a bore!"

She jumped to her feet and wiped her hands on the sides of her skirt. "If you had asked me, I would have told you about the time a pack of wolves surrounded a wagon train just like ours. They circled it all night, howling, with their eyes red in the dark.

At dawn they attacked. They ate every single child on that train under the age of fifteen. Girls first!"

With that she turned and ran off into the darkness between the wagons.

Kate stared after her, shivering a little. Surely Tildy was just making up stuff again. But the wolves were more convincing than the dozens of brothers. She stared into the darkness beyond the wagon looking for glimmers of red. She only saw the campfires of the other travelers and heard soft laughter and the cry of a baby.

Tildy's story was ridiculous. Where were the mothers of those children and their fathers with their guns while the wolves did all that? Tildy was outrageous, that's what she was. Kate took the stick Tildy had dropped and started poking the fire the same way.

Wouldn't Amy just squeal at the thought of anyone talking in such an outrageous way? The thought of seeing Amy made her eyes burn. Would she ever see Amy again, much less sit with her and giggle and talk while they did needlework? As she blinked hard to make her eyes behave, her father came in from bedding down his stock. He called to her mother, who brought Molly out of the wagon, yawning in her nightdress.

It was cozy all being together with Molly chattering quietly to her doll and Kate's parents sitting close together by the campfire. After a while Kate leaned back against the wagon wheel. She wriggled until it didn't poke any place, then shut her eyes. She only halfway listened to her parents' voices.

"We're going to choose a captain when we cross the Kansas River," her father reported. "Once that's done, we'll move along as smooth as cream."

"How can you choose a captain with all strangers?" Kate asked drowsily, thinking of games at school.

Her father laughed. "Folks on a caravan don't stay strangers very long," he told her.

"Didn't I see a little girl out here with you earlier?" her mother asked.

Kate nodded. "Her name is Tildy Thompson."

"Thompson," her father repeated. "Some of the men were talking about him. He's got a whole passel of boys and only that one little girl."

Kate opened her eyes to stare at the fire. She didn't know how many a passel was but it still wasn't dozens and dozens. Come morning she would go and look for Tildy. Even an outrageous friend was better than none.

6
Prairie Grasses

That next morning Kate was jostled awake by the rumbling rhythm of the wagon. She sat up with a start. It was still dark, and Molly was snuffling softly in her sleep. Her father must have lifted them into the wagon and stored the tent as they slept. She heard her mother humming quietly to herself from the seat up front and crawled toward the sound.

Her mother smiled and edged over to make room for Kate. "There's my sleepyhead," she said, her voice whispery to keep from waking Molly.

Kate leaned against her mother and watched the ragged, uneven shadows of the wagons ahead of them. "Why didn't you wake me?" Kate asked.

"The days are long enough without that," her mother said.

"What if I was hungry?"

Her mother laughed softly. "Hungry people wake up," she told her. "I made extra meat and bread for you. You can eat it now or wait for your sister."

By the time Kate finished her corn biscuit and fried pork the sun was ablaze behind them, and Molly had begun to talk to herself quietly in the back of the wagon.

"Where's Buddy?" Kate asked.

"Keeping Papa company," her mother said. "Want to join them?"

Kate nodded and braced herself to jump down from the wagon. The grass was still wet with dew and smelled sweet where the wagon wheels had crushed through it. With Buddy at her side, Kate ran alongside the train, stopping once in a while to stare at the wagons and cattle streaming by. She saw no sign of Tildy. The men and the horses were both too big and rough-looking for her to take her chances getting any closer to look.

She picked an armload of flowers, small reddish violets, stalks of yellow mustard weed, and a pale pink flower that looked somewhat like a daisy except for the way its petals drooped. Buddy startled a meadowlark that limped across the grass, dragging one wing and complaining loudly. Buddy would have lunged after it but she caught his neck and dragged him to a stop.

"She's got a nest," Kate told him. "She's trying to lead us away from it." Buddy wiped at her face with his scratchy tongue as if he understood. He didn't, of course, but just repeating the words made her eyes sting with loneliness for Porter. He had explained the bird's trick to her when they were in Grandma Morrison's west pasture back home.

In among the grasses was a pile of stones, a lot of them. They were stacked up high and had been washed white by the rain. Kate frowned as she studied them. This must be a trail marker, she decided. The wagon train had passed within a hundred yards of it. As she watched, a small bright-eyed animal scampered up on top of the stones and sat on its haunches to stare at her. It looked friendly enough but when Buddy, losing interest in what he had been chasing, galloped toward them, it was off in a whisk, leaving Kate still smiling.

The second time Kate took flowers back to the wagon, her mother stared thoughtfully at the stick Kate was carrying for Buddy.

"I have a job for you," she said. "Instead of just jumping around like a spring lamb, go gather dry wood for me. The dew makes the morning fire hard to start."

At first it was fun but Kate tired of the wood search after the first bundle. The groves of trees were all in the distance and the pieces of wood she found lying in the meadow were damp on the bottom with bugs and worms under them. "Is this enough?" she asked her mother.

"For the first trip," her mother said. "Keep gathering; we've a lot of campfires between here and Oregon."

"But I'm tired," Kate told her.

"How do you think your father and I feel?" her mother asked. "We have been dealing with this road and these beasts since long before dawn."

Kate stood staring at her a moment, wanting to argue. She couldn't ever remember hearing her mother complain before. It was almost as if her mother had left her customary gentleness back with the painted houses of civilization. Some of the prairie grasses had sharp seeds that caught on her pantalets and scratched. It wasn't fair that Molly got to ride while she gathered wood.

"Two more trips with that much wood," her mother told her. "Then you can rest. It won't hurt you to be useful."

The afternoon sun was hot. Kate was cross and sticky under her clothes when she left for the third bundle. If *this* was the way it was going to be all the way to Oregon, she could just curl up the way the white grubs did under the dead wood she was hauling back to the wagon.

She was tugging a dead stick from the damp ground when Tildy appeared suddenly out of nowhere.

"I didn't hear you coming," Kate told her.

"I was Indian-walking," Tildy said. "An Indian brave can come sneaking through the grass so quiet that he has his tomahawk in your skull before you know he's even around."

"Stop that!" Kate said angrily, glancing around nervously in spite of herself. Tildy was wearing the same dress. It had a black streak down the left side that looked like ashes, and her bonnet strings were hanging loose. A pale line of freckles was brushed across her cheeks and that stub of a nose. Her eyes, which Kate hadn't been able to see in the dark, were a strange color, somewhere between gray and gold. She was shorter than Kate but sturdier. The nails on her stubby fingers were unevenly broken and not very clean.

"Let me give you a hand," Tildy said, kneeling to tug at the limb Kate had been trying to get loose. It came all of a sudden. Tildy rolled backward on the ground on her behind. Instead of getting up, she sat where she had fallen, grinning up at Kate.

"A real fighter, that one," she said. "Want to hear about the others?"

"The other what?" Kate asked, suspicious that Tildy was fixing to spin another whopper.

Tildy swung her arms and came to her feet all in one motion, then wiped her soiled hands on the back of her skirt.

"The other girl children like us," she said. "I spent the day scouting."

"I wanted to look for you but there were so many men and horses," Kate told her. "Then my mother made me work."

Tildy nodded, then frowned at the bundle of wood

51

under Kate's arm. She took off her belt, looped it around the wood and handed it back to Kate. "There," she said. "That'll make easier carrying."

With the bundle swinging between them, Kate kicked through the grasses looking for wood as Tildy talked.

"There's one girl with the Hammer wagon. She's got stiff curls and a blue dress and is riding along beside her daddy on a spotted pony. She has a couple of little brothers, too, but they seem decent enough. You wouldn't catch that one out here gathering wood. I called to her. She thinks I don't know she saw me before she looked away, but I did."

Kate stared at her. "Why would she do that?"

Tildy shrugged. "Maybe she thinks she's the queen of something. We can manage without that. Then the Brainards have a girl, maybe two. I only saw one that looked eleven or twelve." She frowned a minute. "I haven't made up my mind about her yet. She could be a brown rabbit."

"What does that mean?"

"You've never seen a rabbit?" Tildy asked.

"Of course I've seen rabbits," Kate told her. "I must have seen a million of them today in this silly meadow. But I don't know any human rabbits."

"You know how rabbits freeze when you look at them and pretend they're not there? She's like that. She's either so stuck-up she can't even stand herself, or she's shy."

Kate wondered how Tildy would describe *her* but was afraid to ask. "Then there's a girl I haven't seen," she went on. "Simon saw her this morning when he went for water. He came back carrying the bucket with one arm behind his back. When I asked him why, he said some half-pint girl like me had talked his other arm off. She's a Parks, he said."

Tildy grinned as she said this and added, "Simon's always trying to be funny. Sometimes he even is."

"Is he one of your dozens of brothers?" Kate asked.

"He's one of the twins, the oldest one."

"How would you describe me?" Kate asked.

Tildy shook her head. "It's your turn to talk. First you tell me how you'd describe me."

Kate stared at her. It would be rude to say her clothes were dirty and she didn't pay any mind to herself, and she'd never known anyone before who told her when to talk.

"Come on," Tildy said. "Speak up."

Kate stared at her, then leaped suddenly with both hands toward Tildy's face and cried out "Yaaah!" the way she did when she wanted to scare Molly.

Tildy's eyes widened and she jumped back with her mouth open. "What in the world?"

"You've done nothing but try to scare me ever since that first night," Kate explained. "Wolves, and Indians with tomahawks in my head!"

Tildy roared with laughter. "That's rich!" she said. "That's really rich."

"Now you tell *me*," Kate said.

"Let's just say that you're wonderful easy to scare."

Kate giggled. She had asked for that. Kate had all the wood she could carry even with one bundle tied in Tildy's belt. She turned to catch up with the wagon, and Tildy ran alongside.

"Take your choice whether you believe *this* or not," Tildy said. "But in just one more day we're coming to a river with cliffs as a high as a church. There's no human way a man can get a wagon across except if he can fly or let it down with ropes like a bucket in a well."

With that she set off, running stiff-legged across the prairie grass toward the front of the train.

"Your belt!" Kate called after her. "Don't you want your belt?"

In answer, Tildy held up both arms and danced wildly for a minute to show that her dress wasn't likely to fall off. Kate looked after her, shaking her head. She halfway wished she had come right out and told Tildy that she would describe her as "outrageous."

7
Harsh Words

The name of the river was Wakarusa. Kate's father walked ahead with some other men to study the terrain. He came back frowning.

"Something the matter?" Kate's mother asked.

"There's a river up ahead we hadn't counted on."

Kate scooted off the seat and slid into the tightly packed back of the wagon. "Want me to hand you out the rope?" she asked.

He glanced at his wife, then stared at Kate. "Exactly what does that mean, young lady?"

Kate was suddenly flustered. "Just something I heard," she told him. "That you either had to fly that river or let the wagon down like a bucket into a well."

"Tildy?" her mother asked.

Kate nodded and hefted the first pile of rope out to her father.

"That little Thompson girl didn't by any chance give you flying lessons, did she?" he asked with just an edge of irritation in his voice.

Before it was over, Kate herself wished she could fly. Everything had to be unloaded from the wagon and carried down the hill. The path was steep and winding with loose stones that tumbled against Kate's ankles when they tore loose and went thumping downhill. After her third trip down, with her ankles aching and her arms wanting to fall from their sockets, Kate was put in charge of Molly.

Molly clung to Kate, throwing her off balance. Finally she let Kate take her arms and lead her down with her eyes shut all the way, whimpering like a hurt puppy.

Once on the riverbank with Molly, Kate stood indecisively. Her father had told her to come back up for more things. That was fine, only was Molly really to be trusted there by the river?

The Thompson wagon was just starting to float into the stream. The oxen, with their heads drawn high and their eyes white with terror, struggled chest-deep in the muddy water. Seeing Kate, Tildy jumped free of the back of the wagon, barely landing on the muddy bank. Even then the tail of her skirt dragged in the water.

"This your sister, then?" she asked, looking at Molly curiously as she twisted the water out of the back of her dress. "She's sort of cute, isn't she?"

Kate shrugged. "She's sort of a pest, too. I need to go back up for more things."

Tildy shielded her eyes and looked up the cliff to where Kate's mother and father were setting out boxes and trunks on the ground. She turned toward the wagon and shouted, "Hey, Simon!"

A young man's head appeared at the back of the Thompson wagon. When he saw Tildy, he yelped, "What are you doing over there? Get back in this wagon."

"My friend needs help," Tildy told him. "You know, the scaredy-cat one."

Kate felt herself flush. So *that* was how Tildy had described her! Well, she didn't need any help from anybody who called her names.

"What you need, Kit?" he asked, looking Kate straight in the eyes with a genial, amused expression. He looked about Porter's age but was taller and broader across his shoulders. His richly colored brown hair was pulled back with a thong of leather, and his mouth turned up a little at the corners as if he had been born laughing.

"Take the little girl," Tildy called, swinging Molly up in her arms to hand to him.

The distance was too far for him to reach. Without hesitation and before Kate could protest, he jumped from the back of the wagon and waded to them. To Kate's astonishment, Molly went into Simon's arms without question, gripping him around the neck as if he had been Porter.

"Easy there," Simon laughed, wagging his head. Then he looked up the cliff. "There's only your pa to get all that stuff down?"

"And my mother and me," Kate said, nodding.

"Sam!" he yelled. A second head appeared at the back of the wagon. "Come on out here and give the Alexanders a hand."

Sam was the match of his brother in size and coloring but he looked shy, as if a smile might come harder to his lips.

"Oh, you don't need to do that," Kate protested, finally finding her voice.

"He knows that," Simon said, hitching Molly onto his hip. "See you on the other side." With that, he disappeared with her behind the canvas flap of the floating wagon.

With Sam and Tildy toiling behind her, Kate climbed back up the cliff, half scared of what her parents would say about handing Molly off to a stranger like a bundle of wet wash. The moment she neared the side of the wagon, she forgot this concern. Her mother and father didn't even sound like themselves. They were almost shouting at each other in tones that Kate had never heard them use before. She stopped where she stood, unable to believe her ears. It was bad enough that they were carrying on like enemies, but to have Tildy and Simon hear them brought a hot flush of embarrassment to her cheeks.

"Be reasonable," her father was shouting, his voice loud and angry. "Think how much those things weigh. Sooner or later we're going to have to dump them. We might as well be shut of them right now."

Her mother, her dark eyes flashing, stood right up to him without flinching. "Those cooking pots are going with me all the way that I go," she said hotly. "And that's the end of that."

"How can you be so bull-headed?" he asked. "You want to back out of the whole enterprise because of a handful of cooking vessels? Can't you see this isn't going to work?"

Kate's stomach twisted into a painful knot. What was happening to her parents? Was this trip already changing them into strangers before her very eyes? She was too embarrassed to look at Tildy and Sam but she shouted to her father, trying to drown out their angry words.

"Papa," she called. "It's me. I brought help."

Her father, his face dark with anger, appeared at the front of the wagon. He glanced at Tildy and Sam behind Kate and frowned as he shook his head. "Oh, no," he said. "I can't ask you to help me."

"Nobody asked," Tildy said. "Sam and I are offering. We'll just help get the stuff down. Give Kate and me something heavy between us; we're strong."

At Sam's nod of agreement, Kate's father glanced back into the loaded wagon. His tone softened. "I'll find some way to make it up," he said. He looked embarrassed. "I *am* in a sort of a bind."

With these words, he disappeared into the wagon to return with an iron kettle filled with cookware. Sam carried Kate's trunk under one arm and Molly's under the other. Kate and Tildy swung the baled iron kettle between them as they started down. Two more trips and the wagon was light enough to swing down the incline on its ropes.

Not until the wagon was solid on the ground at the base of the cliff did Kate's mother remember about Molly. She did this in a shriek.

"Molly!" she wailed. "Where's my baby?" She looked around in panic at Kate. "What have you done with your sister? Quick, where is she?"

Before Kate could answer, Molly called out, "Over here, Mama," from the other side. Kate's mother gasped and clasped a hand to her chest. Kate didn't recognize her sister at once. She was perched on the shoulders of a giant man. She had put his leather hat on top of her bonnet, but it still drooped low enough to almost cover her face.

"What have you done, Kate Alexander?" her mother asked furiously. "What do you mean just passing that child off among strangers?"

"That's no stranger," Tildy told Kate's mother. "That's my paw. Paw likes us girls. He says he don't know what he ever did to God that he got sent so many boys."

Once on the other side, Kate's mother regained

her poise and took Molly from Bull Thompson's arms. "I'm Jane Alexander," she told him, offering her hand. "I just got panicked there for a moment. I don't know how to thank you."

"You and Dan had your hands full," he said genially. "It's not going to kill a man to help."

It took two days for the caravan to work its way to the shores of the wide Kansas River. Once there, the men built two huge canoes, which they laced together with a platform of poles. Slowly, one by one, they rolled each wagon onto this raft and towed them all across by hand. The cattle swam, which they didn't really want to do, and the rest of the travelers crossed by boat.

Five days passed before the whole train made it across the river. It was almost like a party. Kate saw a lot of children she hadn't really noticed before. The Applegate family had nice boy cousins who looked to be about ten. They ran and shouted in endless games through the prairie grass. Some of the children weren't that pleasant. One gang of little boys ran with a leader named Tom Patterson. Tom made Kate think of Jeb Haynes with his bullying ways. He and his buddies sneaked up on little kids and scared them with Indian calls. They shouted dirty names at the girls and threw stones at the cattle. Even good-natured Simon Thompson got cross with the Patterson boy. "That one's spoiling for a fight," he told Kate. "Chances are he'll get one."

The men who weren't working with the cattle or the ropes on the river went hunting every day. The women washed clothes, hung them to dry, then stood in little knots to visit.

Kate's mother came walking back from the river's edge with a tall woman and a young girl about Kate's age. Kate saw the girl's stiff curls hanging in front of her ears and down her back and guessed it must be the Hammer girl.

Kate's mother was good with introductions. The girl's name was Dulcie, and her family came from Ohio, too.

Kate tried to think of something to say after "Hello," but nothing came. That turned out to be all right because Dulcie spoke up right away. "Are *you* twelve yet?" she asked.

Kate shook her head and then remembered to speak up. "I'm still only eleven." She didn't have to admit she had only been *that* since right after Christmas.

"Then you must be *just* a sixth-grader," Dulcie said with satisfaction. "*I* was in *seventh* and at the *top* of my class."

"My friend Amy was at the top of *my* class," Kate told her, since that was the best she could do. She was terribly distracted by the way the girl talked, coming down on some of her words very hard as if she were afraid you would miss something she said.

"Have you met *Pansy Parks* yet? She's about *your* age. *Then* there's Peggy *Brainard*."

"And Tildy Thompson," Kate said.

"I've *seen* her," Dulcie said, looking away for a moment as if to clear her eyes of the memory. "I thought *the four of us* should get together and *do* things."

Kate wanted to remind her that there were five of them but was somehow afraid to. Unlike Tildy, Dulcie didn't wait for her to take her turn talking. She played with the ribbons on her dress as she talked with her voice bouncing from word to word in that important way. Her fingernails were so smooth and shiny that Kate turned hers in and made little fists so Dulcie wouldn't see them. She'd totally wrecked her hands pulling that silly wood out of the dirt.

"There are *lots* of things we could do, like *sew and read books*, or maybe play *games. I'm* going to *press flowers* in a book *all the way across the country*. That way *I'll* have them to remember *the trip* by."

"That would be nice," Kate said lamely. She felt cross with herself. Why hadn't she thought of that? She'd only picked those flowers and left them on the wagon seat to die. Now she couldn't make a pressed flower collection without being a copycat of Dulcie. She'd thought right at first that Dulcie was pretty, but when Dulcie talked she leaned forward a little

63

with an eager, wide-eyed look that made Kate feel that Dulcie was going to pounce on her. And she looked too dressed up to be going to Oregon.

"I'd *even* help you with schoolwork if you wanted to *keep up with it,*" Dulcie said, smoothing her dress.

Kate's smile hurt her face by the time Dulcie and Mrs. Hammer walked off toward their own wagon. Kate's mother glanced at the sky. "Look at that! Past noon already. Run find me some wood for the fire, Kate, and I'll make a good supper."

"What about all that nice dry wood I already gathered?" Kate protested.

"I'm saving that for a rainy day," she said.

"I'll bet Dulcie Hammer doesn't gather wood," Kate grumbled.

"That's *her* mother's problem. Now scoot!"

The fire was already crackling when Kate's father came back from hunting. He beamed with pride as he handed over some fat prairie hens and a brace of young rabbits.

The smell of the prairie hens browning in hot fat was so rich and delicious that Kate couldn't stand it. When the hens were steaming under the cover of the big iron skillet, her mother dropped dumplings into a pot of stewed rabbits with onions. "You mean, you cooked all that meat for one night?" Kate asked.

"Indeed I did," her mother said. "I'm glad you're back. I want you to go tell Tildy's mother not to bother fixing dinner. This rabbit stew will be done in good time for her meal."

"I don't know where their wagon is," Kate protested.

"Then go find it," her mother said. "She and her brothers didn't have any trouble locating our wagon when we needed help."

Kate went away feeling somehow bruised. When had her mother gotten so bossy? She never used that tone with Kate back in Ohio. Didn't she know it was scary to walk among the wagons and have people stare at you as if you had no business there?

Kate kept one hand on Buddy's neck as she walked among the campfires. The men had gathered to talk about the election. She heard words like "captain," and "sergeant," and "council." The raw smell of whiskey sometimes overwhelmed the scent of cooking food. On one fire an antelope was roasting on a wooden spit.

She passed the Thompson wagon without knowing it, but Simon called out to her. "Hi, Kit, looking for Tildy?"

"Actually," Kate said, looking up to where he sat in the seat of the wagon mending a boot with an awl and a steel needle, "I have a message for your mother."

Simon stared at her, then jumped down. He glanced back at the wagon and led her away a little into the long grass. He wasn't exactly whispering but he kept his voice so low that nobody in the wagon could have heard him.

"Tildy hasn't said anything to you about Maw?"

Something in his voice chilled Kate and she shook her head.

His hand on her shoulder felt the way Porter's used to when he "had a talk" with her.

"Well," he began, "you see, Maw's gone and Tildy don't much like to talk about her."

"Gone," Kate breathed. The very word made a hard lump in her chest. What did "gone" mean? Was Tildy's mother dead? The thought brought a quick rush of tears to her eyes. And if she wasn't dead, where was she? Kate remembered her own mother's words back at the Wakarusa River: *Those cooking pots are going with me as far as I go.* Could Tildy's mother just have had enough and gone back?

"It ain't much fun for women . . . or men," Simon said. Then he patted her shoulder. "Maybe I can take your message."

"Supper," Kate blurted out. "Mother made a stew for your family for tonight."

He stared at her. "What made her do that?"

Kate stared at him. "Papa got rabbits and — " She paused. "I think it's her way of thanking you for your help."

"That's a real lady you got for a mother," he said. "Wait'll I tell the boys. Do I need to come get it?"

Kate nodded. "It's in that big iron kettle."

He nodded and winked. "The one your folks had a spat over?"

She wanted to say her folks didn't spat but he had heard them. "It'll probably be ready in about an hour."

"You tell your maw she's a princess," he said, winking again.

Kate didn't give her mother Simon's message. Neither did she tell her that Tildy's mother was gone, because she wasn't sure how the words would come out. When she said Simon would be over later, her mother nodded and smiled.

Sam came with Simon to get the kettle, and they brought it back later, cleaned out and dried.

Simon grinned with that smiling mouth at Kate's mother. "Paw says to tell you that you cook as pretty as you look and he's much beholden."

Kate's mother waited until Sam and Simon disappeared behind the wagon, then turned to Kate. "You spend a lot of time with Tildy," she said. "What does beholden mean?"

"I think it means he owes you something," Kate told her.

"Oh, but he doesn't," Kate's mother said, looking at Kate's father with a funny, angled glance. "There'd be no decent stew for anyone ever without those boys of his."

That night, when the election was over, Kate's

father was as full of talk as Molly usually was. He talked about the Applegate brothers, Charles, Lindsay, and Jesse, and their big families and big herds. One of the Applegate men had been made a captain. Tildy's father, Bull Thompson, and her own father had been put on the council of nine. A doctor named Marcus Whitman, who had been over the trail before, was to serve as guide.

The name "Whitman" was enough to make Kate cry herself softly to sleep. It reminded her of her Uncle Whitmer Morrison, who was a doctor, too. All of a sudden she hated him. *He* had lured Porter away from them to go down to St. Louis to study doctoring. They had barely started and already they seemed so far away. Would she ever hear Porter call her "Moppet" again?

8
The Gosling Drowneder

Kate had always liked rain. Her own bedroom back home in Ohio fitted in under the eaves. Unless a rain was carried by wind, she could even leave her window open. The sheets of water poured from the eaves like a veil of icicles between her and the wet world. Rain had its own music, a drumming on the wooden shingles, a chiming through the metal downspouts.

The rain that began just on the other side of the Kansas River was different. The sullen downpour fell from curdled clouds that looked low enough to reach up and touch. The soil melted into a slough of mud too liquid to support the weight of a wagon. The oxen strained mightily to turn wheels that were buried to their hubs.

Even if the wagon train had moved at a sensible speed, this wasn't a storm one could pass through. It hovered over them day after day as they slowly followed the trail that ran along the Little Blue

River. Kate told herself it had to get better because it certainly couldn't get worse.

Maybe the storm didn't get worse, but the tempers of the travelers certainly did. Men who had been genial friends shouted furiously, threatening each other with remarkable punishments.

Kate's mother, seeing that her daughter listened wide-eyed to these exchanges, frowned sternly. "Best you close your ears to that blasphemy," she told Kate. "The words of angry men are not for such as you."

Although Kate nodded her understanding, her mother knew as well as she did that such lively language stuck in one's mind like cockleburrs to knitted stockings. She repeated some of the phrases over to herself to be sure she wouldn't forget them. Sometimes the words themselves made no sense, but the way they were said made Kate collapse into giggles. As serious as the men were about their anger and the awful things they meant to do to each other, they still sounded a lot like Jeb Haynes and the boys "talking dirty" behind the school outhouse back in Ohio. If she ever saw that Jeb Haynes again, she knew things to say to him that would make his hair stand up straight!

The men of the train had split into two factions. Farmers like Kate's father who had only four cows following his wagon, complained bitterly that the "cow men" such as the Applegates and Bull Thompson, who were moving great herds of cattle west, were slowing their progress. They argued that the train should split so the farmers could move ahead at some sensible speed. And indeed the cattle seemed to have no great urge to see Oregon. They stopped to graze or stare across the dripping prairie until they were set to moving again by whips and angry shouting.

Every morning the guide set out early with a handful of road builders who marked the route with little flags. At the same time they picked the places the train would stop at noon and again for the night. It made sense to Kate for someone to pick places to stop at noon and night, but the trail already seemed marked by those mounds of piled up stones.

All day long Kate dreaded the time when the train would stop for the night. It was a slow and painful process to get the wet, muddy wagons drawn into a great circle. The wagons were placed to face outward with their tongues tied together. The cattle milled about in the center to keep them from being rustled by the Indians. All night the miserable cattle lowed a chorus of complaint that sometimes even drowned out the yapping of the coyotes in the distance.

Kate had complaints of her own. They couldn't use the tents because the water ran in streams along the soaked ground. Except on the nights when her father drew guard duty, the whole family had to crowd into the packed wagon to try to sleep. Day after day they had nothing but cold food because no fire would burn in the constant downfall. The air smelled like moldy cheese and Kate's skin was red and chafed from wearing wet clothes.

The best times were when she and Tildy huddled together on a wagon seat and talked. Actually Tildy didn't do much of the talking, Kate realized. Instead, Tildy asked her over and over to tell stories of how it had been back in Ohio. Before Kate knew it, Tildy knew all about her grandparents and Aunt Agatha, her school (and Jeb Haynes) and her friends. Kate wanted to know about Tildy's mother, but didn't know just how to ask. Tildy did like to talk about Kate's mother.

"I think Jane is just the best name ever for a mother," Tildy told her. "It's so ladylike and gentle, just like your mother really is."

"You've never told me about your mother," Kate reminded her. "Does she have a pretty name, too?"

"That depends," Tildy said.

"Depends on what?" Kate asked.

"Depends on whether you like it or not," Tildy said, her tone turning cross. "If I wanted to talk about my maw, don't you think I would do it?"

"You don't care what I want to talk about," Kate told her. "You only want your own way all the time."

They rode a while in silence before Tildy spoke quietly. "Maw's name is Belle and her hair's as

crinkly as yours only lighter. She dances as ⌐
a thistle, but only when she's happy."

Kate sat very still, her head boiling with q⌐
tions. Where was this mysterious Belle, and how
could she be happy when her own daughter Tildy
sat scrunched down in a wagon, missing her so
much that her face wrinkled into knots thinking
of her?

"I hope she's happy now," Kate said quietly.

"She made her choices," Tildy said. "Now tell me
more about this Amy person. Tell me again how she
looks and dresses and what games you played and
what you talked about when you two were together
back there."

"You don't really take proper turns," Kate complained. "You tell me a tiny bit, then I have to tell
you a lot."

"I don't have such interesting things to tell," Tildy
replied. "I've never had a girl friend."

"What about me?" Kate asked, struck with the
note of sadness in her tone.

"You're probably only my friend because we're
traveling together," Tildy said.

Kate frowned into the sheeting rain. "All right,"
she agreed. "How do you think Amy and I got to
be friends? It was only from living down the road
from each other. Friends are people you get to know
because they are around. If you don't like them, they
stay acquaintances or neighbors."

"It's still not the same," Tildy said in a gloomy tone.

"Are you saying I couldn't choose Dulcie and Peggy and Pansy on this trip?" Kate asked.

Tildy stared at her a moment, then smiled that wonderful gap-toothed way. "You could!" she said. "You really could."

When they turned west along the side of the Platte River with the dark skies still holding, Kate's parents got even more snappish with each other. Mostly they just didn't look at each other, but sometimes their feelings boiled out into words.

Kate's mother had finished her morning work. Tight-lipped, she'd milked the cow and made breakfast. The cream from the day before swayed in a bag from the buckboards to churn itself into butter from the jiggling of the wagon bed. Her father was still struggling to harness the oxen for the day when Duke stepped back, driving her father's boot into the mud with a sharp hoof. Kate's father yelled and shouted out a great stream of those words Kate had been told not to listen to. Kate's mother stiffened angrily and glared at him.

"I'll have you remember, Mr. Alexander, whose idea this journey was," she snapped. Even Molly was silenced by this. Kate caught her breath, half afraid of what might follow. She'd never heard her mother call her father anything but "Dan" before.

"And I'll have *you* remember, Mrs. Alexander, that I undertook this journey thinking your son might put his hand to the task with me. We would have been two men together, instead of one man slaving for a wagon full of womenfolk. It's more than a man can handle to be teamster and hunter and guardsman and husband all at once. And all the time with my belly howling for a decent bite of warm food."

With that, her father turned to the oxen without a backward glance. For the next few hours Kate's mother sat so straight on the wagon seat that Kate thought her back must be like to break. Kate felt a little panicky. What if they had really quit loving each other and were only going to be cross and bark at each other from now on?

Even Molly sensed that something was wrong. Instead of chattering to Annabelle, Molly held her doll close and sucked her thumb the way she had when she was tiny. Kate scooted over and put her arms tightly around Molly. If Kate couldn't understand what was going on between her mother and father, what was a little thing like Molly to think about it?

It was still raining when Kate's mother broke her silence suddenly.

"Kate, put on your oilskins and boots. I have an errand for you."

Her tone didn't invite argument. Kate glanced at

the streaming rain and obeyed. When she was dressed, her mother spoke again, still without looking at her.

"I want you to go to the Thompson wagon for me. Ask one of the boys if he will hunt for me today. Tell him I'll pay him gladly, either in coin or cream or butter, whatever is his pleasure."

"Hunt what?" Kate asked.

Her mother glared at her. "For whatever he can find in this godforsaken wilderness." Kate backed away. For a horrible moment, her mother's voice had sounded exactly like her Aunt Agatha's.

The mud was near the top of her boots by the time Kate slogged her way to the Thompson wagon near the front of the train. Sam was driving the wagon with Tildy at his side. Simon walked alongside, leading the oxen.

"Hi, Kit," Simon called to her. "What are you doing out in this gosling drowneder?"

When she stared at him, he laughed, swung her up, and crowded her onto the wagon seat beside Tildy.

"Do you know what a gosling is?" he asked.

When she nodded, he laughed again. "When you get rain enough to drown a young goose, you've got a gosling drowneder. Now, what's up?"

He frowned when she relayed her mother's message. "What does she have in mind, eating raw meat?"

When Kate admitted she didn't know, he looked thoughtful. "Your Maw and Paw didn't have another one of those spats, did they?"

How in the world had he guessed? His tone was light, as if such a spat were funny. It *wasn't* funny at all, but she didn't want to make a fuss about it. Since Simon had heard them yell at each other before, she might as well admit it. "A little one," she said. "I think Papa's just overworked." As she spoke, she wished she believed her own words. Just being overworked shouldn't make you cross with someone you loved.

"Where are the rest of the boys?" Tildy asked.

"Out herding with Paw," Simon told her. Then he patted Kate's shoulder. "I'll get Carl up here to help and go out myself."

"I'm a better shot," Sam called up to him.

Simon laughed. "You are at that, but I'm quicker to see game. I'll get Carl and Titus both." He glanced at Kate. "Want to ride with Tildy for a while, or do you need to go back?"

"I'd love to stay," she said, grinning at Tildy. "But the way things are, I'd better get back."

"I could come along," Tildy suggested.

"That would be great," Kate said. "But you'll need cover from the rain."

Tildy tugged a shawl from behind the seat and pulled it over her bonnet. "I'm neither sugar nor salt," she said.

Simon swung both girls down. As he set Tildy beside Kate, he pinched her cheek. "I say you're sugar," he said softly.

For a sudden, blinding moment Kate's eyes filled with tears that ran hot among the cold raindrops on her face. Porter used to say things like that to her, too. She remembered how warm his hands were when he swung her off the fence onto Bridie, and tweaked her cheek, calling her "Moppet." She missed him so much that the inside of her chest hurt. It wasn't fair for Tildy to have all those brothers, when Kate was so alone with only Molly and her parents snappish at each other.

"What's the matter?" Tildy asked, staring into her face as they started toward the wagon.

"I miss my brother," Kate admitted. "I miss him something awful."

"Take one of mine," Tildy said airily. "Anyone you please. You like the twins? They generally like to stay together. Sam's a little on the quiet side but Simon's fun. You don't really know the others, do you?"

Kate shook her head, a small, crazy idea rippling into her mind.

"Buck is the oldest," Tildy rattled on. "He's a little rough-talking but a power of a man for only twenty. Carl's next and he's more like Sam than any of the others. He's a wonder with a fiddle and can sing birds out of trees. Then there's Jackson, who can make anything in the world that can be made by a man's hands. And Titus."

"How come you didn't describe Titus?" Kate asked.

"He's strange," Tildy said. "Nobody can describe Titus. Most folks wouldn't try. Best I can say is that he's more like Maw than any of us, a pure dreamer with his head off someplace in the stars."

The crazy idea had grown until it completely filled Kate's mind. "Listen, Tildy," she said breathlessly. "I can't just *take* one of your brothers, but maybe Papa could hire one — or even the twins. That way he wouldn't have to do guard duty at night and work with the oxen all day, too. Maybe he'd get his good humor back if he was more rested."

"Could your paw afford to do that?" Tildy asked. "If not, they might help out sometimes from just good hearts."

"Papa wouldn't stand for that," Kate told her.

"Pride goeth before a fall," Tildy reminded her.

Having Tildy in the wagon made the morning pass quickly and cheerfully. Tildy made Molly laugh by holding her doll and pretending to talk for her in that funny, gravelly voice. Before Kate knew it, it was nearing time for the noon stop. Simon rode up to the side of the wagon, and grinned up at Kate's mother.

"Would you say an antelope was too big?" he asked her.

"An antelope!" she cried. "They run like the wind." Simon laughed and gestured with his head to Sam following slowly with the animal drooping behind his saddle. Both the boys and their horses were dripping, but even silent Sam was smiling with pride.

"You're wonderful," Kate's mother cried. "I want to pay you. What do I owe you?"

"We talked that over," Simon said, keeping that laughing mouth as straight as he could. "If you can cook it in this rain, we'll take what your family doesn't need." His laughter bubbled up so he couldn't go on for a minute. "If you *can't* get it cooked, we get to watch you eat it raw."

Kate's mother laughed so merrily that Kate saw her father glance over at her for the first time that morning.

"The price includes dressing it," Simon said. "That's going to mean we drop back, but we'll catch up at the nooning place."

As they rode off, Kate's mother began to give orders. "The minute the wagons begin to stop, you jump down, Kate. Look for stones, the biggest you can find. Get a bunch together, enough to stand up off this infernal mud."

"I'll help," Tildy offered quickly. "But rain falls on stones, too."

"I believe you're right, Tildy," Kate's mother said, smiling. "I do believe you're absolutely right." Kate's mother leaned and touched Tildy lightly on the cheek and smiled. Tildy caught her hand and held it tightly a moment. Something in her friend's face made Kate's heart ache. Maybe Jane Alexander hadn't been her old sweet self on this trip but she had *been* there, mothering Molly and herself. The thought of traveling day after day without her mother made Kate's shoulders tighten.

Molly piped up into the silent, awkward moment. "Talk for my doll, Tildy," she begged.

Tildy stuck her hand inside the doll's dress from the back and waggled her arms and began to sing "Yankee Doodle," keeping time with the doll's arms.

The morning dragged away, and still Kate's mother and father weren't speaking. This was the longest they had ever stayed mad. Sooner or later, one of them usually smiled and started talking softly to the other. Kate was really scared by the time the wagons stopped for nooning. What if they never made up? What if all the burdens of this trip had killed their loving each other the way deep winter killed tender trees?

The minute the wagon stopped, Kate and Tildy jumped down and started on the rock pile. Even though a bunch of the other travelers stopped to stare at the pile of rocks Tildy and Kate collected a few yards away from the side of the wagon, Kate's father only gave quick, sharp glances their way. When one of the men asked what the girls were doing, Tildy, carrying a great flat rock with both arms straight because of its weight, glanced at him.

"Making a rock circle so we can have an Indian rain dance," she told him soberly.

He laughed and quit asking but watched with the others.

Kate's mother brought out her umbrella and a bundle of the dry wood Kate had gathered clear back in Missouri. By the time the fire caught and the smoke was feeding out from around the edges of the umbrella into the drizzling air, she had set the iron skillet on the fire to warm.

The Thompson boys had cut the antelope flesh into long, thin strips. "The fastest way to cook it is on a spike held over the fire," Simon told Kate's mother. "I don't figure you'll need the skillet."

"I've got the skewers ready," she told him. "The skillet's for bread." She handed the umbrella to Kate. "Here," she said, "you keep that rain off the fire. I'll be right back."

Kate's father, who had taken the oxen to water and set them to graze, came to the fire while his wife was still clattering inside the wagon.

"You boys bring in that antelope?" he asked. "What a wonder you are. I'm ready to pay a pair of good hunters."

"We already bargained with your wife," Simon said.

As he spoke Tildy jabbed Kate hard with her elbow. "Now," she whispered. "Make your deal now."

Kate, with the cool side of her face turned away from the fire and blinking furiously to keep the smoke from her eyes, turned to her father. "Papa," she said, suddenly needing to clear her throat. "Sam and Simon made a deal with Mama on the hunting, but I expect they would hire on as teamsters if you thought you could use them."

He stared at her a moment without speaking. Behind him, the iron skillet hissed as Kate's mother poured in a full measure of bacon grease. They all turned to watch as she laid an inch-thick circle of dough in the pan and covered it quickly.

"Papa, listen to me," Kate insisted.

Instead, he turned to speak to Simon and Sam. "I know your father needs your help."

"He has dozens of sons," Kate said. "Simply dozens. He won't even miss them."

Simon laughed and knelt to thread the strips of meat on the skewers Kate's mother had put down on the stones. The smell of the rising soda bread in the skillet, and the rich scent of the roasting meat, made Kate quiver with hunger.

"That Tildy has a tongue like a running horse. I'm not sure she's the best influence on your Kit," Simon said, grinning up at Kate's father. "But Paw doesn't need all of us, really. He just keeps us working to hold us back from mischief. Sam and I would be proud to help out."

For the first time since morning Kate saw her mother's and father's eyes meet. Neither of them smiled, but her mother spoke to her husband in a truly pleasant tone.

"Dan, I'd much appreciate it if you'd lift this skillet lid for me so I can turn the bread."

Kate's father was swift to her side. Simon winked broadly at Kate, as if to tell her not to worry about her folks. Then he turned to Tildy. "Scat off and get Paw and the others. Tell them if they want some hot roasted meat, to get down here and help cook it."

9
The Separate Ways

Every morning the night stars still shone when
Kate jerked awake to the sound of gunfire.
Someday, maybe, she would quit leaping like a
frightened rabbit when the guards woke the camp
with that awful salvo of rifle shots. That day sure
hadn't come yet. She didn't even want this day,
anyway. She wanted this whole entire trip to be
over. The rain had finally stopped, leaving mud pud-
dles of loose dirt to dry and blow all day long. How
could Oregon possibly be worth the getting to, if the
getting there only went from miserable to boring
and back again like a seesaw?

Outside the tent her father called, his tone
brusque and impatient. "Coming," she answered.
Even if it was evil and disrespectful, and a secret
she had to hide in her innermost heart, she didn't
like Papa as much on the road as she had liked him
at home. Even with the Thompson twins helping
him every day, he still wasn't the same genial person
he had been in Ohio.

Could she ever make a list of things she didn't like! She didn't like it that the wood was gone. She could gather the big flat chips of dried buffalo manure as well as the next person, but she didn't like it. She didn't even like eating bread and bacon cooked over the smoldering piles.

She sat very still a moment, just staring. No matter where she was or what she was doing, she was never comfortable and relaxed anymore. When she curled in the tent at night she heard the distant howling of wolves, and the skin crawled on her back. She couldn't even go for a walk without watching out for snakes. Tildy had taught her to recognize the looping, ropelike pattern that the side-winding rattlesnakes left in the dirt and sand. And if the dangers of the wild weren't enough to worry about, she had to watch out for Tom Patterson and his miserable friends. If she got careless and got caught alone, they chased her and threw buffalo chips at her. The chips hit hard and were painful. Sometimes they broke when they hit and left dry nasty threads tangled in her hair.

But a lot she could do about anything! She shook Molly's shoulder in the darkness of the tent, then made a face at herself as she pulled on her dress. There was something else she didn't like. All her clothes smelled nasty, a mingled scent of dust and smoke and sweat. She would almost trade her breakfast for a nice hot bath. Her Grandmother Morrison had a copper tub that she filled with steaming water scented with lavender. But what good did it do to think about that?

"Come on, Moll," she coaxed, tugging her sister to her feet.

Molly was as limp and manageable as her wooden doll, Annabelle. Kate dressed her in minutes and nudged her out-of-doors so the tent could be taken down. Cook fires sent thin columns of smoke into a sky streaked with dawn. The earth beneath Kate's feet trembled from the rhythmic beat of horses' hooves. Never mind that the riders were men; they acted like boys first thing in the morning, racing each other to bring in the great herd of cattle that hadn't spent the night inside the wagon circle.

The circle of white gleaming wagons was already being broken as men hastened to untie their wagon tongues and yoke their oxen. Kate was glad to see that her father had King and Prince already in place and was shouting and shoving to get Duke and Earl lined up behind them. A late start would mean that all of them ate dust all day.

Kate shook her head to clear it of dreams. If it hadn't been so early, she would have loved the excitement of it. All around her, tents were being struck, wagons loaded, and frying meat scented the air. Bugles trumpeted wildly over the din.

Kate's breakfast didn't have time to make it into her stomach before it was seven o'clock. The wagon train swung into line in platoons of four. The order of wagons varied from day to day so the same families wouldn't get the dust every day. Her father never made it to the front of the line, but then again, he never brought up the rear as the true laggards did.

Molly had leaned against her mother and fallen asleep again, her mouth half open and her hands curled palms-up in her lap. Not even the unhappy, bawling cow herd jostling along beside and behind the wagons disturbed her.

Kate didn't mind the cows but she was sick to death of hearing the men shout at each other. Mostly they fought about the big herds of cattle. The farmers, who felt the cattle herds were holding them back, kept saying they were going to split up the train and go on alone. Kate didn't believe this could happen. The reason for a big wagon train was that they could all protect each other. The arguments became so bitter that the more hotheaded men didn't stop at words but threatened each other with weapons and dire punishments. Sometimes they even swung their horses out from the train to dismount and batter at each other with their fists.

"Why do men always have to fight?" Kate said in irritation, more to herself than anything.

"It's the general misery," her mother said without even looking her way. "There are too many of us; too many beasts, and too many people."

"Those who don't like it ought to go back," Kate grumbled. When her mother laughed, Kate looked at her with suspicion. She hadn't *meant* to be funny.

Her mother stared straight ahead. Her voice seemed to come from a distant place. "If that were the rule, there wouldn't be a woman left in this whole train."

Kate stared at her mother's profile. "You mean *all* these women just came because their husbands wanted to?"

Her mother nodded. "Most of us go with our husbands and stay with them, in sickness and health, in good times and bad."

Kate pulled her lip down. "That doesn't seem fair to me when it isn't what you want to do."

The expression her mother turned to her was mingled with astonishment and annoyance. "Kate Alexander, I can't believe what comes out of your mouth. A woman — no, any adult — doesn't spend her life doing what she wants to do." Kate cringed at her tone. "Do you think it's *fun* to be tired and dirty and sore all the time? No sane woman ever chose to bump along a trail month after month, worried to death for fear that her loved ones get sick, or hurt, or fall prey to the dangers of this trackless wild!"

When her mother fell silent, Kate stared down at her hands in her lap. She should probably feel ashamed but she wasn't. All her life she had been preached to about obedience and duty and loyalty, and she knew what the words meant. But words didn't make it fair that a woman had to give up her own dreams and be miserable because of somebody else's.

She was relieved when the silence between them was broken by Tildy shouting her name.

Tildy was off to Kate's right, running alongside the train. Every few steps she leaped up, waving both arms in the air. "Can I go with Tildy?" Kate asked, suddenly cheery at the sight of her outrageous friend.

"Not too far from the train," her mother cautioned. "Stay where I'll have you in sight."

As Kate jumped down, Buddy bounded up to wash her face with good morning. She shoved him away, then caught him in a hug.

"Take him along," her mother called. "I'll feel better about you."

She and Tildy weren't the only children who chose to stay clear of the boiling dust from the wagon train. A pack of little boys stalked each other through the tall grass, while another band shouted and brandished sticks in a mock war. The lucky ones who had ponies raced them madly in advance of the train. Dulcie Hammer and her two constant companions walked sedately along beside the train. Dulcie seemed to be reading aloud to Peggy Brainard and Pansy Parks.

Tildy stared idly at the three girls as she waited

for Kate to join her. Kate followed her glance. "Dulcie is probably teaching them school," she said. "She offered to help me with lessons the first time we met."

"It must be nice to know so much," Tildy said in that funny, rough voice that Kate had learned to like. Then she grinned at Kate, showing the little gap between her teeth. "What do you want to play?" Tildy's eyes looked more gold than gray in the early light and her freckles had paled to a faint butterscotch color.

"I guess we could pick flowers," Kate suggested without much enthusiasm.

Tildy shook her head. "We've done that to death." She frowned and kicked at a grass clump with a scarred boot. The grass plant flew from the loose sandy earth, exposing a pale tan root.

"That's it," Tildy cried with excitement. "Let's play we're Granny Annie."

Kate stared at her. "What in the world is a granny Annie?"

Tildy's eyes glistened. "She's an old woman back home. I mean she's *old*. She's so old that her nose has curved down almost to her chin and she's got no teeth in between. She's possum old and coon smart, Paw says."

"What makes a coon so smart?" Kate asked.

"You're changing the subject," Tildy said. "Don't you want to know how to play Granny Annie?"

"Of course I do," Kate said.

As she spoke, Tildy knelt and pulled the weed the rest of the way out of the ground, blew the dust from the root, and studied it. "Now this," she said, "is nothing I've ever seen before. Therefore it is nothing." She tossed it away airily. Buddy galloped after it, took it between his teeth and brought it back to her. She threw it again, farther this time, and turned to Kate. "Every day when Granny Annie has her breakfast eaten and her dishes washed up, she goes out and fills her apron with things she digs up."

Kate studied her. This had all the earmarks of another wild tale. Tildy sensed her doubt and protested loudly.

"Granny Annie is real. She collects wild things to eat, and to heal, and to dye yarn with — just the way Indians do. I bet we could fill your apron by nooning."

"How would we know what to dig?" Kate asked, doubtful. She *did* have an apron on but it was her last clean one. Who knew when they would reach water fit to wash clothes in?

"I know a lot of them," Tildy told her. "I learned from going digging with Granny Annie." She fished in her dress pocket and brought out a knife. "We can dig with this."

Kate stared at the sharp blade in horror. "Where did you get that? Why, that thing could have cut right through your pocket and sliced up your leg."

Tildy pulled her mouth down in disgust. "Simon lent me the knife in case someone gives me a hard time. Only a fool could get hurt with a sheathed knife in her pocket. Now, do you want to go play dainty with that Dulcie Hammer or do you want to play Granny Annie with me?" she asked.

"You'll have to show me what's worth carrying back," Kate said.

Tildy frowned at the prairie grass a moment, then grabbed Kate's arm. "Come on. I see something already."

They dug a long time, filling Kate's apron with goldenseal roots, wild licorice, wood sorrel, and sarsaparilla root.

"I'm tired," Tildy finally announced. "Now it's fun time." She plumped herself down in a bed of red clover. Nobody had to tell Kate what that was. Porter had taught her to suck the honey from the tiny petals of the clover flower before she was even Molly's age.

Kate lay flat on her back, drowsy from the sun and the sweetness in her throat. She was half asleep when Buddy whined and leaped to his feet. She called to him without opening her eyes. Instead of obeying, he barked and took off at a gallop. Tildy shaded her eyes with her hand then jumped to her feet.

"He thinks something is wrong over in that copse

of willows," she said. "Let's follow him."

"But the end of the train is going by," Kate protested, staring at the back of the last wagons with a sudden sense of panic.

"Buddy says something is wrong," Tildy said, starting off toward the trees running. "Come on."

Kate's heart began to thump hard. "Leave him be and he'll come," she shouted. "We have to catch up with the train." What was the matter with Tildy? Didn't she know that Buddy could have flushed a bear or a panther? There might even be Indians. The grove was shaded, mysterious, and threatening. Worse than that, the last of the laggard wagons had passed. She and Tildy were alone with the wolves and the snakes and dangers of the endless prairie.

Tildy hadn't even looked back. "I'm going to leave you," Kate yelled, fighting sudden tears. What could she do? What *should* she do? She couldn't leave Tildy to whatever kept Buddy barking frantically along the trees, but she couldn't just let the cattle rumble by and ever hope to catch up again.

Her fear made her angry. "I'll drag her," she told herself furiously, tying her apron in a knot to keep the roots in. "Dumb, dumb, dumb," she shouted through her tears as she ran toward the grove. "That Tildy is dumb and crazy and pigheaded."

"Hurry," Tildy shouted as Kate drew nearer. Only then did Kate hear a child's sobs in between Buddy's anguished yelps. Tildy was kneeling beside a tear-stained little boy. He was filthy with dust and had wet his knickers. He looked to be about five and his face was streaked with channels where the tears had run.

"What's the matter?" Kate asked.

"His foot's caught in this root," Tildy said. "I can't get it out the way he's wiggling."

"He *has* to get it out," Kate wailed. "The train has gone past. We're all alone out here."

The minute Kate touched his ankle, the child gave an anguished yelp. "Maybe he's sprained it," she suggested.

The boy nodded, spilling a fresh flood of tears over his muddy face. "Unfasten his boot," Kate told Tildy. "Then we can get his foot out and jerk the boot off."

"That's smart," Tildy said, working the boy's pale, thin foot out. The boot came off with a brisk tug.

Panic made Kate's voice wavery and strange. "We've got to go. We've got to catch up."

"Can you walk?" Tildy asked the boy, frowning at the wagons now growing smaller in the distance.

He shook his head violently. Kate caught a deep breath and glanced again toward the wagons. It would be hard enough for her and Tildy to catch up without having this boy to haul along. It was strangely quiet now that even the herd had passed. Only a few head of cattle and the last of the outriders were still passing.

"Never mind that," Kate snapped at her. "We'll have to carry him. I haul Molly sometimes. We'll take turns."

It would have been easier if Kate hadn't been so scared. The boy was heavier than he looked, making Kate stumble on the rough ground. The boy himself was a mess. He clung to Kate's neck and snuffled wetly on her shoulder like a sick kitten. She gasped for breath and called for Tildy to take her turn. Instead, Tildy started running across the grass toward the last of the outriders just galloping by. She was shouting at the top of her lungs and waving her apron full of roots in a big circle over her head.

Kate stopped as a rider swerved his horse to gallop toward them. When Kate recognized Tildy's oldest brother Buck, tears of relief poured down her cheeks and she staggered under the boy's weight. Buck was there in seconds, dropping from his horse to stand at Tildy's side. He didn't seem to be a boy at all but a genuine man, broadly built with a dark-bearded face under the shadow of his wide-brimmed hat.

"You crazy little tykes," he said, his tone really angry. "Do you want to get yourself killed? What are you doing out here all by yourselves?" Then he saw the child clinging to Kate.

"Who's the pup?" he asked, turning to Tildy.

"The little Hammer boy," Tildy said. "He trapped

his ankle and banged it up. He's full heavy for Kate and me to carry."

Buck knelt and smiled full into Kate's face. Then he set his broad brown hand on her shoulder. "I'd say that was fair." He turned to the boy. "What do they call you?"

"Jake," the child snuffled.

"Then let's ride you home, Jake," Buck said. He lifted the boy and set him in front of his saddle horn. "Up with you rascals, too," he said, swinging Kate up first and then Tildy.

They crossed the prairie like the wind with Buddy racing along beside them, lolling his tongue with delight at the chase. As Buck pulled up beside the wagon train, a woman came running, clinging to her bonnet with one hand and squealing wildly.

"My baby!" she wailed. "My son!"

Dulcie was only a step or two behind her mother, limping on the soft leather shoes that Kate had envied at their first meeting.

Buck slid from the horse and handed the wailing child to his mother. Dulcie drowned him out. "I didn't look away a *minute*," she cried. "He was there and *gone*, just like *that*."

When Mrs. Hammer set the child down, he let out a great shriek from the pain of his weight on his ankle. Mrs. Hammer pulled him against her tightly. "What have you done with little Jake? How did he come to be riding with you?"

"Kate and my Tildy found him trapped in a thicket," Buck told her, his voice very deep and calm in a warning way. "He was too heavy for the girls to carry back."

"Don't tell me that," Mrs. Hammer said furiously. "Little Jake would never wander off. He just wouldn't have gone. You must have lured him off."

"Ma'am," Buck said, trying to interrupt this flow.

"Don't argue with me. Clearly you lured him. No Hammer would follow a ragamuffin like your sister away from camp. Anyway, his sister was watching him."

"Every *minute, Mama*," Dulcie put in. "Every single *minute*."

Buck listened with a cold expression on his face. Then he tried again. "Ma'am," he said once, then repeated the word increasingly louder until the startled woman stared up at him in amazement.

Jake spoke into that moment of silence. "Nobody took me. I went," he said. He burst into fresh tears and pressed his face against his mother's skirt.

"He *couldn't* have. I was *watching*," Dulcie said. "Anyway, what does *he* know, he's *only four*."

Buck stared at Dulcie with an expressionless face. "The train could have passed on and the wolves got to him first," Buck told her in a level tone. "An Indian might have chanced by and thought he was worth taking for ransom. There are even snakes."

When Dulcie began to wail as lustily as her

brother, Buck turned back to the mother. "I suggest you teach that young lady to stand up for the truth. She's already proved she can lie like a trooper." At that he tipped his hat, jumped on his horse, and galloped back toward the rear of the train.

After supper was over Mrs. Hammer came to the Alexanders' fire with Dulcie at her side. She stood a moment with her head bent as if she had to force her words out. "I understand from my Jake that he might owe his life to that fine wolfhound of yours," she said. "I do want you to know how much his help and that of your daughter means to me."

Kate's mother was splendid. She took the apology with a genteel nod of her head and asked about the boy's injured ankle. While they talked, Dulcie stood very straight with her curls all in place and her hands twined delicately in front of her apron. She smiled brightly at Kate.

"Have *you* heard the *news*?"

Kate, fuming with fury, could only shake her head. Dulcie *couldn't* know anything that Kate wanted to hear.

"The men *voted* just before supper. The farmers are going to *go on ahead*, and leave *us cattle men* to follow at our slower pace."

Kate nodded. That wasn't big news. The men had been arguing about it ever since they crossed the Kansas River.

"I really *envy* you," Dulcie went on. "*You* and your family can get there sooner and *you* won't have to *put up* with those *trashy Thompsons* any longer."

Kate stared at her in disbelief. For the first time it struck her that if the train split, her father would be in the group that moved ahead, with the Thompsons following behind. But that couldn't be! She couldn't bear this trip without Tildy. And how could anyone, even Dulcie Hammer, say such rude and thoughtless things in such a ladylike tone?

"I don't *want* to leave my friend Tildy," Kate said, not caring that her voice sounded funny and strangled.

Dulcie widened her eyes as if she could hardly believe her ears. Then she shrugged very elegantly. "*Well*, they do *say* that *birds of a feather* flock together."

"And so do pigs and swine," Molly piped up quickly.

Dulcie's mouth dropped for a moment, then she straightened both her back and her face. "*That* is the *rudest* thing I've *ever* heard in my *life*," she said with a little tremor in her voice.

Dulcie's own words about Jake echoed in Kate's head, and she said them aloud, almost as she had heard Dulcie say them.

"What does she know? After all, she's only four."

When Dulcie turned and walked away, her mother glanced after her, then hastened to follow.

10
The Queen of the World

The minute Dulcie and her mother left, Kate broke into Molly's prattle to ask about her father.

"He's at the meeting with the men," her mother said. "He could be late getting back. Come give me a hand with getting this tent up."

Kate hated helping with the tent. The ropes had been wet so many times they left her hands smelling musty, like mildew. Stiff hemp strands jumped loose and tore at the skin of her palms. For once it didn't matter. The thought of losing Tildy made her heart so heavy that nothing else really mattered. While Kate pulled the ropes tight around the stakes her mother drove into the ground, Molly squatted by the fire talking a blue streak to her doll. Buddy, on his haunches beside her, seemed to be listening with high interest, now and then twitching an ear at her change in tone. On Kate's last trip out of the wagon with bedding, her mother glanced at her thoughtfully. "Is something the matter, Kate?" she asked. "You don't look like yourself."

Kate shook her head. She knew if she tried to talk to her mother about not seeing Tildy any more, she would cry.

"Lean over here," her mother ordered. When Kate obeyed, her mother pressed her hand against Kate's forehead and then in under her ears. "Does your head hurt? Is your throat raspy?" her mother asked with concern. "You don't *feel* feverish."

Kate only shook her head again.

"I don't like the way you look." Her mother's tone betrayed her concern. "Maybe a good night's rest will help. You tuck into bed there with Molly and try to get to sleep."

"But I want to see Papa," Kate protested.

"You'll see him in the morning," her mother said briskly. "Into bed with both of you."

Going to bed was one thing, getting to sleep quite another. Kate felt that she had been there half the night before she heard Buddy leap to his feet and bound off with a low, happy whine. That would be her father. She thought about risking her mother's anger and getting up, but decided against it. In her heart she already knew that Dulcie had probably been right and the rest of the way west would be dull and boring and lonely. She cried quietly to herself until she *did* have the headache her mother had worried about.

Her father was standing by the fire with his coffee cup when she crawled out of the tent the next morning. She didn't even say "Good morning," but only blurted out, "Dulcie told me the train is breaking up."

Her father nodded. "The men decided that late yesterday afternoon. Now maybe we'll have some peace along this trail."

"What's going to happen now?" she asked, holding her fists tight against her sides.

"Well," he said. "The train will break up in the next few days. The split was almost even with sixty-one wagons planning to pull out ahead. That leaves about the same number of wagons to follow along with almost three thousand head of cattle. The men with the big breeder herds elected Jesse Applegate as their captain last night. He's a good choice since he and his brothers all have big herds."

Her father hunkered by the fire with one arm around Buddy and took a piece of hot corn bread from the skillet.

"How long do Tildy and I have?" she asked.

He stared at her. "What are you talking about?"

In spite of herself, Kate's words came out in a wail. "Papa, I'm losing my best friend in the whole wide world. I need to know how many more days we have together."

"Kate!" her mother cried, leaving the fire to come

and put her arms around her. "Oh, my dear. You must have thought you were losing your little friend. I thought you'd guess that we would stay with the cattle train."

Kate pulled back to stare at her, and then at her father. "Papa, do you mean you're not going to cut away with the other farmers?"

He grinned at her. "What? And lose my two good helpers? I don't know where I'd be by now without those Thompson twins. You bet I'm hanging back with the cattle men, and glad to have the chance."

Kate cupped both hands over her mouth to keep from squealing with joy. At the same time such quick tears of relief filled her eyes that she had to blink hard to make them go away.

"I'm sorry you had all that worry," her mother said, touching her shoulder lightly. "Why didn't you ask?"

"I was afraid to hear," Kate admitted. "Oh, Papa, I'm just so happy." She wanted to run and grab his neck and hug him as she had in the old days, but the cooler habit of the trail held her back.

His smile was the old one. "Happy is how I like to see my girl," he said quietly. "And we'll be just as safe. The cow column will try to stay close enough for mutual assistance if need be."

Traveling northwest across the Kansas plains was wonderful. It *was* more peaceful after the train separated. Kate and Tildy ran through sweet-scented grasses spangled with wildflowers. Molly trudged along filling her little bucket with colored stones, which she discarded the next day in favor of new ones.

Herds of antelope, startled from their grazing, seemed to flow across the grasses. The air was riotous with bird song. Kate liked the meadowlarks best. Their song went straight from her ears into her heart, making it sing, too. Rosy-backed sparrow hawks hovered above the ground, their wings a blue blur as they flailed the air to stay aloft. At night, owls spoke genially from the willow thickets. Once in a while the hunters brought in a buffalo and Kate's mother cooked steaks and made a savory brown gravy.

Sometimes when Tildy ran with Kate, her bonnet slipped off, letting her hair fall like a shining mane down her back.

Tildy's hair was a rich chestnut-brown that she didn't really "fix" any way at all. Instead she just grabbed great wads of it and stuffed it inside the full back of her bonnet.

One morning she arrived breathless at the Alexander wagon. "Who's chasing you?" Kate asked, watching her friend pant for breath.

"Paw," Tildy gasped. "He almost caught me, too."

"What did you do?" Kate asked, remembering

how Porter used to chase her down when she tried to run away from punishment.

"Nothing," Tildy's tone was enraged. "I was behaving as good as gold, cooking soda bread for breakfast, when my bonnet fell loose. Paw said he wasn't so bad off that he had to eat hair in his food and swore he'd cut mine off to some reasonable size. I thought he'd forgotten but when I got the kitchen stuff put away, he came out with his razor."

"Cut off that beautiful hair!" Kate cried. "He couldn't. He wouldn't."

"He can and he will if I don't keep it back tidier."

"That's easy enough," Kate said.

"Look who's talking with all that curl. Straight hair worms out of everything."

"Not braids," Kate told her. "Why don't you braid it?"

Tildy flushed scarlet under her freckles. "Maybe I don't know how."

Kate grinned at her. "At last there's something I can teach *you*. Have you a comb?"

"Back at our wagon," Tildy said.

"I'll get mine," Kate said. It was only a minute's work for Kate to hitch herself up into the wagon and return with her own brush and hand mirror. "Let's run ahead so Mother can keep her eye on us. Then we'll sit and I'll braid it for you."

"That won't teach me much."

"After I'm through, I'll teach you with grasses.

There's some knack to it but it's not hard."

Tildy eyed the brush with suspicion. "You won't pull now?"

"I may have to," Kate told her. "There's ever so many rats' nests in the back. But once they're out, you can keep them out. Come on. I'll race you to the front of the train."

Tildy won, but as Kate caught up, Tildy was staring back down the train. Kate turned to see Dulcie, Pansy, and Peggy high-stepping into the prairie grass with baskets over their arms. "They *would* choose today to come out," Tildy growled. "What are they going to think of my not doing my own hair?"

Kate giggled. "They'll be jealous. Who else has a lady's maid?"

Tildy was a good sport. She hardly complained at all, except for an occasional groan when Kate had to tug hard to get a knot out. The train moved slowly past them. Dulcie and her friends stared openly as they passed a few yards away.

"Maybe *next* she'll get a *bath*," Dulcie piped in a tone clearly meant to be overheard.

"I'm going to slap her face," Tildy warned, trying to jump to her feet.

"No such thing," Kate said, hanging onto Tildy's hair tightly. "You'll sit right here and let me finish."

"Then can I look in the mirror?" Tildy asked, folding her hands back into her lap.

Kate stood back to look at her handiwork. "It's beautiful, simply beautiful," she cried.

"Not burdened with modesty, are you?" Tildy asked, reaching for the mirror.

"Not my braiding, your hair," Kate explained. "Feel it, it's as glossy as silk and just as shiny."

Tildy stared into the mirror as she stroked the smooth plait hanging halfway down her back.

"Don't you like it?" Kate asked when the silence seemed to go on and on.

Tildy nodded, and choked out. "It *is* beautiful," she whispered. "And it's mine."

"Now," Kate ordered. "Pick some strong grass, as long as you can find. We'll need three bunches."

At first the grass strands seemed to slither from between Tildy's fingers. She bit her lip and frowned darkly at the strands as if to scare them into cleverness. She walked along slowly while Kate gathered bachelor buttons and ox-eye daisies along the way. When Tildy wore out the first grasses, Kate handed her the bouquet. "If you braid these together, you can make a garland."

"Garland?" Tildy asked.

"Like a necklace to put over your blouse," Kate explained.

By the time they had almost caught up to the Alexander wagon, Tildy had braided a strand of blue and white flowers almost long enough to trail to the ground.

"Now tie the ends," Kate told her. She ran ahead and called up to her mother. "Wait'll you see the beautiful thing Tildy made."

Her mother turned on the seat and looked back. "Tildy!" she cried. "Get up here where I can see you. You are beautiful indeed." With Tildy on the seat beside her, Kate's mother lifted the gleaming braid and let it drape over her hand.

"Tildy, it is glorious," she said. "What a beautiful rich color it is, and how it catches the sunlight. A woman's hair is her crowning glory. Look!" She wound Tildy's braid into a shining crown on top of Tildy's head and laughed softly. "What a little lady you are, my dear!"

Tildy's round cheeks flushed with color and her eyes shone. She looked as if she were about to burst with happiness at Kate's mother's praise. She had clasped her hands so tightly around the garland that she was crushing the flowers before she remembered.

She thrust the garland into Jane Alexander's hands. "Kate meant the flowers," Tildy said, her husky little voice rougher than usual with emotion. "See, it's a garland."

"It's beautiful, Tildy," Kate's mother said. "It's fit for a queen. Do put it on."

Tildy shook her head, the shining braid swinging. "It *is* for a queen," she whispered. "I made it for you."

With the garland around her neck, Kate's mother held Tildy close and hugged her for a long moment. Kate felt such a rush of tears to her eyes that she had to look away. How awful, how perfectly terribly awful Tildy must feel not to have her mother! I would die, Kate told herself. I would probably curl up and die.

Molly was only envious. She stared at her mother wide-eyed, and wailed. "I want it, Mommy. I want it."

"This one belongs to your mother," Tildy told her. "I'll braid one for you."

"And Annabelle, too?" Molly asked, holding up her doll.

Tildy laughed and jumped down beside Kate. "One for you and Annabelle, too," she chanted. Then in a whisper to Kate, she added, "Remind me never to dicker with that sister of yours. She drives a hard bargain."

Dulcie and Pansy drew near as Kate and Tildy picked daisies and bachelor buttons for Molly's garlands. Dulcie stood holding her basket in both hands, watching them.

"Look what I have, Kate. I have seven different flowers already," she said. "Those two and five others."

"That's very nice," Kate said without looking up.

"Why are you just picking daisies and bachelor buttons? They're so *common*. They grow *every-*

where. I am collecting new and different flowers."

"That's *very* nice," Kate said, wishing she would go away before Tildy got so sick of being ignored that she started something.

Dulcie did seem to be losing interest. She frowned a little, staring across the grasses. "Look, Pansy," she cried. "There's a brand-new one there. The orange flower."

Kate and Tildy both looked up at the excitement in Dulcie's voice. The orange flowers were indeed beautiful. They grew on a plant almost buried in shrubbery. The orange blossoms were tiny and star-shaped, set in a dense flat-topped cluster on a tall stalk that stood at least a foot tall.

"Butterfly weed," Tildy mumbled to Kate. Then she leaped to her feet and started running toward Dulcie, shouting. "Stay away from that. Be careful."

Dulcie turned, her eyebrows high in disdain. "*Who* are *you* to tell *me* what I can pick or cannot pick?" At that, she plunged into the thicket to reach for the flower.

Tildy froze at her tone. "It's too late, anyway," she told Kate quietly. "Let's take our common flowers and our common selves back to the train."

Kate had to run every few steps to keep up with Tildy's swift pace. Tildy's voice was hoarse with anger and resentment. "That Dulcie Hammer really thinks she's something. Queen of the World, that's who she thinks she is. She better never ask me again who I think I am or she'll find out. I'll give her two good ears full and maybe a bloody nose to boot."

"I don't understand," Kate said. "What was wrong with that flower?"

"Nothing," Tildy grumbled. "It was where it was growing."

"I still don't understand," Kate admitted, catching up.

"Just remember that I warned her," Tildy said. "I gave her every chance in this whole world that she's queen of. Now, let's braid garlands."

11
Flying Bears and Stars

Kate felt as if they had trailed along beside the Platte River forever. Somehow the Platte didn't even seem like a single river at all. It looked more like a family of rivers that wandered along cordially together. Sometimes the streams drew near to each other and sometimes they swung apart. When the sun caught the water's surface the land looked as if a child had festooned it with silver-blue ribbons.

At least this part of the trip wasn't boring. Sometimes great clouds of dust rose above the distant dark mass of a racing herd of buffalo. Sometimes when Kate and Tildy ranged away from the train to gather buffalo chips, they even saw Indians. Usually they had only a swift glance at a band of young men on fleet horses. Late one afternoon Kate stared after such a disappearing band wistfully.

"Just once I wish I could see an Indian up close," she told Tildy. "Not a scalping one, of course, but a young girl one like us."

"If you did, she'd probably have a baby tied up in boards on her back."

Kate stared at Tildy hard. "Are you going to start in on those monster fibs again?" she asked.

Tildy straightened to look at Kate eye-to-eye. "That's not any kind of fib. They tie their babies in bundles and carry them around like that."

"How do you know so much about Indians? You've never gone westering before, any more than I have."

"I've done it in my mind," Tildy said. "And I've listened."

Kate was tired of the subject. She was even tired of the day. The afternoon air had become so hot and heavy it was hard to breathe. Little rivers of sweat trickled down her back under her camisole and she itched all over. "Let's go back to the wagon train," she said. "I'm sick of looking for chips."

Tildy's whisper came low and raspy. "Stay still for a minute and don't move. You got your wish." As she spoke, she nudged Kate hard in the hip.

When Kate looked up, she shivered in spite of the heat. The Indian boy was only a few yards away. How had he come so close without her hearing him? He stood very still, studying them both with dark, thoughtful eyes. For a crazy moment she thought of Amy. Would Amy believe her if she said she saw a boy their own age, naked except for beaded slippers and a little leather apron? Amy would swear she made it up. But somehow he looked all right without clothes, because his skin was a rich deep color that made the necklace of teeth on his bare chest almost shine.

Kate gripped her chip basket so hard that the handle creaked from the pressure of her fingers. He mustn't know how wildly her heart was thundering. And she smiled at him just from nervousness alone.

Tildy, at her side, stayed silent and unmoving.

The boy kept his eyes steady on Kate's for a long moment, then he smiled, too, a tight, closed smile that turned the sides of his mouth down instead of up. Then he suddenly lifted the bow with his right hand and waved it in the air. Kate jumped a little at this unexpected movement, and felt a fresh wave of fear shudder through her bones. Was he giving a signal to some one hiding? Kate's knees softened and she felt like dropping.

He made a funny sound, not a word but not quite a grunt, either, then shook the bow again and waggled his head vigorously. Beside her, Tildy gasped. "Look!" she cried, "he wants us to *look*."

When Kate turned to look, she hardly believed her own eyes. In those few minutes the sky had darkened in the distance. The blue was altogether gone in the southwest where the very earth seemed to be rising upward in wavering, dark gray pillars.

"Twister!" Tildy shouted. "Let's get home!"

Kate grabbed the basket close to her chest so she could run faster and glanced again at the boy. He was nodding at them, as if in approval. "Thanks," she called to him, smiling another one of those quick, nervous smiles before she turned to run. After a few minutes she glanced back. He was gone and the darkness had eaten its way halfway across the blue of the sky. She saw a widening funnel spin along the horizon. Although it was black and forbidding, it swayed as gracefully as a dancer poised on one slender foot.

The outriders had seen the coming tornado, too. They galloped behind the great slow-moving mass of cattle, shouting and spinning their lassos, trying to tighten the herd and drive it from the path of the coming storm. Kate only glanced at them and kept running through the consuming darkness toward the wagon train.

Tildy's scream came suddenly over the rising whine of the wind. "Stop, Kate, stop!"

Tildy had thrown away her basket and was running toward Kate full-speed with her arms widespread. Her eyes were white all around with terror as she yelled, "The cattle, Kate! The cattle!"

When Kate looked back, she gasped. The outriders had more than stirred the cattle herd to motion. Their shouts, combined with the howling wind, had thrown the giant herd into a stampede. The beasts were moving at a gallop in one flowing, thundering surge north and west in the direction of the wagon train. Another few yards and Kate and Tildy would have been caught in the path of their wild flight.

"Run, Kate, run!" Tildy screamed, grabbing Kate's arm and shoving her backward toward where the Indian had been.

Tildy *couldn't* mean for them to run directly toward the swaying blackness of the tornado. "The twister!" Kate yelled, to remind her.

"RUN!" Tildy repeated, hauling Kate along. Kate stumbled and fell, then fought her way to her feet again, one knee aching and her left elbow wet with blood inside her sleeve. Her eardrums seemed about to burst from the howling of the wind and the drumming hooves of the herd coming steadily nearer. Whatever she was breathing into her chest couldn't be air because it hurt too much.

They raced toward a mangy cluster of willows along a dry streambed. As they reached the first of the trees Kate went down again. This time she didn't fall. Tildy caught her by the arm and dragged her down so roughly that Kate cried out with the pain in her shoulder.

"The ditch!" Tildy yelled. "Jump into the ditch."

The streambed was lined with rough gray rocks and cluttered with dead tree limbs and the skeletons of tumbleweeds. Kate was too terrified to protest. She rolled over the stones, trying to shield her face from the clawing dry branches. She was dead. She was at least as good as dead. The cattle were right on them. Too winded even to bellow, the frantic beasts seemed to be gasping and snorting right in her ear. The rhythm of their hooves vibrated from the ground, shaking her whole body. Tildy gripped her arm painfully.

"On your belly!" Tildy shouted. "Cover your head."

Too terrified to think, Kate numbly obeyed. She had somehow lost her bonnet during her flight. Her bleeding elbow stung as she folded her arms over her head and pressed herself against the floor of the gully.

Just when she expected the first hooves of that pounding stream of cattle, the herd separated, taking a split path around the grove of trees.

They were there and then gone swiftly, leaving a curious hollow silence in their wake. Even the howling of the wind abated, leaving the air heavy and foul with the dust raised by the passing herd.

"Tildy," Kate whispered after a minute. "Is it over?"

"Don't move," Tildy said. "Just wait."

From somewhere Kate heard cattle bawling and the shrill terrified nickering of horses. Then, almost delicately, the first slow pattering of rain began. The downfall quickened to a torrent almost at once. Within minutes water coursed along the streambed, swirling among the rocks, spinning weeds along on its surface.

"Now," Tildy said, taking her arm. "Now we can get up."

Kate hurt too much to get up. She ached all over and the raw scratches on her arms and face stung. Her shoulder throbbed when she tried to lift herself.

Tildy had risen to her haunches to stare into the darkness after the retreating storm. It was a dwindling blackness in the northeast, a blanket of horror still whipping its way across the prairie.

"We've got to get out of here before we drown," Tildy said, scrambling to her feet. "That was some kind of fool luck. That thing went almost straight over us."

The rain pelted Kate's face, making it hard to breathe, much less to speak. "The wagon train," she gasped, peering in the distance. "I can't even see the wagon train any more." With her words came realization. "Mama!" she cried, leaping to her feet. "Papa! Molly!"

Neither the cattle nor the wagon train were any longer in sight. The dim horizon was only littered with debris, fluttering white canvas and piles of lumber tossed here and there as if a giant had played at jackstraws.

Tildy stood beside Kate peering into the darkness at the distant destruction. Over the hammering of the steady gray rain came the anguished bellowing of wounded animals. Suddenly, as if she had been struck, Tildy dropped onto the wet earth and covered her face with her hands. Kate knelt and put her arms around her.

"We're all right, Tildy," she said. "Don't cry. We're all right."

Tildy's body jerked with great compulsive sobs as she clung to Kate and she shook her head vigorously. When she finally spoke, it was a question. "Where's Maw?" she wailed. "Where's my maw?"

Kate had never seen anyone cry that painfully. She didn't know what to do, except hold her friend and wait for the storm of grief to pass.

Tildy's sobs lessened slowly. Finally she sighed, dragged herself to her feet, and swiped her hands across her wet, dirt-blackened face. "We'll be all right, Kate," she said, her voice tired and lifeless. "They'll be looking for us, and I want to see my paw. You just wait and see. Somebody will come."

The prairie that lay between them and the battered wagon train was littered with wounded cattle and uprooted trees. How could anyone even see them in the darkness under this starless sky?

"How do I know the wolves won't find us first?" Kate said. "You wait all you want. I'm going to walk."

"We'll have to go slow," Tildy told her. "Something hit my knee powerful hard and it hurts to put my foot down."

"Then we'll go slow," Kate said, taking Tildy's arm. Kate couldn't bear to look around her as they slogged through the rain across the prairie. The dead cattle were bad enough, but the wounded ones broke her heart with their helpless bellowing. Every few minutes they had to stop and shove the mud from their boots in order to lift their feet.

"Want to sing something?" Tildy asked suddenly in a strangely loud voice.

"Sing!" Kate cried. "What's the matter with you? I've never been so miserable in my whole life." She rubbed her muddy hands on her skirt. "I'm cold and wet and filthy and I hurt all over."

Instead of answering, Tildy began to sing in a loud quavery voice. Only when she caught her breath did Kate hear the other new sound, a distant howling, now and then broken by sharp barks.

"What's that?" she asked, grabbing Tildy's arm.

"That's why I was trying to sing," Tildy snapped at her. "To keep you from talking about being scared. Scared is catching and I don't need it."

Kate walked in silence for a moment. "Why should the wolves eat us when they have all this dead meat?" She turned to stare at Tildy. "How did you know what we should do back there? Did you have twisters in Kentucky?"

"Once in a while," Tildy said. "I never saw one but I've heard a lot of talk. We had luck getting in under that one. Did you ever see that bear that got whipped up into the sky?"

"I don't need any whoppers."

"This is for real. Come a clear night you can see a whole bear that went flying up into the sky and got outlined with stars."

Kate grunted. Let her talk if it made her feel any better. Flying bears *were* better to think about than the barking of the coyotes that seemed nearer with every step.

"Then there was this funny thing that happened to an old lady," Tildy went on. "She was knitting in her rocking chair when a twister carried away her house, lock, stock, and brick chimney. When the neighbor men came rushing to see how she was, she snapped at them something awful for making her lose track when she was counting stitches."

Kate glared at her. "I don't think that's funny, and anyway, how could that be?"

"Hush," Tildy said, listening. Kate heard nothing new except distant bellows and the shrill whistle of a night bird. Tildy was silent a moment, then she put her muddy fingers against her teeth and let out a piercing whistle that Kate felt slice through her head.

"What are you doing?" Kate asked angrily, clapping her hands over her ears.

Tildy didn't answer. She was jumping up and down and laughing wildly. "Here!" she shouted. "We're over here!"

An answering shout came from the darkness along with the sudden sound of hoofbeats. Simon was off his horse and at Kate's side in a moment. He pounded Kate on the shoulder and shoved Tildy so hard that she reeled against Kate. Then he gathered them both against him and held them tight for a silent minute.

When he spoke, his voice was gruff. "Come aboard, you scamps," he said softly. "I'll even give you a ride home."

Simon's horse cantered warily over the littered prairie, dodging the swift streams and animal carcasses. "Is everybody all right?" Tildy asked as she and Kate clung to Simon's warm, wet back.

"We were lucky," he told her. "And Kit back there, too."

Tears coursed down Kate's cheeks as she leaned against Tildy's back. Hurting didn't matter, nor cold, nor wet. As they drew nearer to the wrecked wagon train, a child was screaming and women were crying. Even if the wagon was gone her mama would be there along with Papa and Molly. She couldn't let herself think about Tildy sobbing out there in the ditch for a mother who *wouldn't* be waiting.

12
Brown Water and Pink Roses

Kate's mother couldn't even speak. She only held Kate tightly against her and cried. Molly caught Kate's arm and clung to it as if she never meant to let go. "Papa?" Kate asked. "Where's Papa?"

"With the cattle," her mother said. "The men all rode out with the herd in hopes of settling them by morning. He wanted to come look for you but the twins talked him out of it. Simon said he and Sam had the best chance of finding you and Tildy."

Kate remembered the piercing whistle out there on the prairie and nodded. She was starving. Huddled under oilskins in the mouth of the wagon, she ate one cold corn biscuit right down and then nibbled on a second one. With Molly slack with sleep, Kate and her mother nestled close and watched the night sky. The endless rain was lit by lightning that came different ways. Sometimes it zigzagged down the sky and left sharp, glowing images that stayed in Kate's mind after the dark came again. Sometimes it was a general glow along the horizon, as if someone were playing a lantern against the line of the sky. No matter how it came, it was followed by thunder that trembled the earth beneath the wagon.

Slowly the rain tapered down to a drumming. Kate leaned against her mother's warmth. "Do you think of home?" she asked quietly.

Her mother nodded silently.

"And wonder if it's the same there as when we left?" Kate asked.

Her mother laughed softly and tightened her arm around Kate. "I know what you're saying, Kate. It *is* hard to believe, after all we've gone through, that life is the same back there as we left it."

"Sometimes I think I imagine things," Kate told her. "Things like the way mashed potatoes taste when the butter melts yellow in a hole in the middle, and how nice it feels to sit in hot water and have your skin smell good."

"And to sleep on clean, dry sheets fresh from the sunny wash line," her mother added. "And people. I know we both miss Porter. And I know you miss your friends, Kate. I certainly do miss mine."

Kate stared at the dripping darkness. Why hadn't she ever thought of that? Of course her mother had friends. And she had left them as surely as Kate had left Amy and the others.

"I'm lucky," Kate told her. "I have Tildy."

Thinking of Tildy reminded her. "Have you ever heard anything about a bear in the sky all outlined with stars?"

"Yes," her mother said, after a minute. "I think there are two, a little one and a big one."

Kate sighed. Two flying bears. She hugged her mother's arm. "I love you so much," she whispered. "Both you and Tildy." Instead of answering, her mother pressed her lips against Kate's forehead, leaving it glowing with warmth.

Several of the wagons were beyond repair. After a great hammering and sawing and not a little cursing, the wagon train was finally ready to set off again, with fewer horses and cattle but no loss of human life. That day, after a cold breakfast and with wet clothing fluttering from the wagon frames, they set off for the forks of the Platte River.

Jake Hammer and Molly had become friends the day he hurt his ankle. Almost every day since, he had hobbled down to the Alexander wagon to play with Molly. That afternoon he came and squeezed into the seat between Kate's mother and Molly. Both of the children were prattling along at a great rate with nobody seeming to be listening. He was a nicer little boy than his sister was a girl. Kate loved to hear him laugh. He had a funny, quick giggle that ended with a hiccup. He and Molly laughed a lot together. For all her jabber, Molly was a lighthearted, happy person to be around.

The weather wasn't happy. The rain fell sullenly all day, as if it felt robbed that the twister hadn't spun them all to kingdom come. When the sky finally cleared, Kate walked Jake through the streams of grasping mud back to the Hammer wagon. The rain made supper late. Kate's mother warmed soup and passed around cold bread. While they were eating, Molly announced that Jake's sister was sick.

"What's the matter with her?" Kate's mother asked with a worried glance at her husband. She was forever feeling Kate's head and Molly's and fretting about one of them "coming down with something."

"Jake didn't say," Molly replied, tilting her bowl to catch the last of her bean soup in her spoon. "He just said she was lying in the back of the wagon with wet rags all over her face and arms and carried on a lot."

"After supper I'll go check on the child," her mother said. Kate felt her mother's glance but didn't look up. She didn't intend to go calling on Dulcie Hammer unless she was dragged there.

While her mother was clearing the supper things away, Kate walked quietly around the wagon and then ran off swiftly to see Tildy.

"I've got news," Kate told Tildy. "The Queen of the World is sick."

"Sick how?"

When Kate repeated what Molly had said, Tildy scrambled into the back of the wagon. After a lot of scratching and thumping, she came back out. She dropped to the ground holding something tied in a rag. "If I'm right, I've got what she needs," Tildy said. "Let's try to catch your mother before she gets there."

"I don't understand this," Kate asked, trying to keep up with Tildy's rapid trot. "What's in that piece of goods?"

"Touch-me-not leaves," Tildy called back. "Come on, hurry."

Kate's mother was just leaving the Alexander wagon as they ran up. "I wondered where you disappeared to so fast," she told Kate, her voice heavy with disapproval.

Tildy was bouncing up and down with eagerness. "Tildy brought something for you," Kate said.

"Touch-me-not leaves," Tildy said, thrusting the bundle at Kate's mother. "They're for that Hammer girl."

After a puzzled moment, Kate's mother asked, "Isn't that what they use for poison sumac? Why do you think that's Dulcie's problem?"

"I saw her pawing through poison sumac to pick a butterfly weed the other day."

"And you didn't warn her?"

"I tried to," Tildy said. "She's not what you'd call good at listening."

Kate's mother drew her mouth down to keep from smiling. "This is awfully nice of you, Tildy," she said. "I think you ought to take it to them yourself. You deserve the credit."

Tildy shook her head so that wonderful braid swung from side to side. "It probably wouldn't even work for them if they thought it came from the Thompsons."

Kate's mother stood staring at Tildy a moment, then touched her cheek gently. "This is very nice of you, Tildy."

Tildy flushed very red and ducked her head. "I take no credit. Fools can't help being fools any more than a skunk can make the air smell like violets."

The wagon trains of the farmers which had gone on ahead had arrived at the fork and were waiting. Kate's father groaned at the scene. The river was no longer strips of silver ribbons but a rolling brown flood, coursing down the southern branch they had to cross to reach the north fork.

"Maybe it's a passing flood," Kate's mother suggested.

Her father shook his head. "Even if it means to pass, we can't take the risk. We still have the mountains to cross before winter. We have to press on."

Both trains made camp. Because of the confusion of animals and people, Kate's father tied Buddy by the wagon and went off with the men to plan the crossing.

Although the water was too thick with mud for any use at all, either drinking or washing, Kate's mother sent the girls to the stream to bring back buckets of it. "After it sits a while, a few clean inches will gather at the top," she explained.

Kate filled her bucket the third time and looked crossly at the foaming torrent of the river. "I don't see how we'll ever get across," she told Tildy. "Look how far it is to the other side."

"Boats," Tildy said. "The wagons have to be turned into boats."

"Sure, Tildy," Kate said, cross because the muddy water kept sloshing on her skirt. "And we'll turn the cattle into birds so they can fly over."

Tildy turned to her with a wide, delighted smile. "That's *good*, Kate. That's really very good."

Kate tightened her lips together. "It's no sillier than making great wagons into boats."

"Why do you think all the hunters went out?" Tildy asked.

"Because they're hungry. Just as I am," Kate told her.

Tildy shook her head. "They went for buffalo. They'll use the skins to make the wagon boxes waterproof. Then they'll take the wheels off and float them over."

Kate stared at her. "Where did you get that?"

Tildy giggled and tried to do her funny little dance, even though her boots made sucking noises as they left the mud. "I listened to the men planning it. But if you can teach the cattle to fly, it would be a great help."

While they were talking, Buddy had begun to growl. Kate turned to see what was wrong. That awful band of boys that ran with Tom Patterson had come up behind the wagon and were hurling stones at Buddy. The dog yelped as a stone struck him. His growl turned to a snarl as he began to strain at the rope, lunging toward his tormenters with bared teeth.

"Stop that!" Kate yelled, setting down her bucket and running toward them. "Stop that this very minute!"

"It's only a girl," one of the boys said. They all laughed and another stone struck the wagon behind Buddy. Kate screamed and ran past them to Buddy's side. She knelt with her arms around him. "All right, you dummies!" she shouted. "I dare you."

The words were barely out of her mouth before the stone struck. It wasn't a big rock but it hit Kate squarely on the shoulder that had hurt since the tornado. She screamed at the pain and clutched Buddy tighter, tears pouring down her face.

The scream was barely out of her mouth before her father came running up behind the boys. Two of them saw him coming and took off running. He caught the Patterson boy by his collar and whirled him around.

Kate cringed at the fury in her father's voice. He shook Tom, cuffed him across the head, and threatened to beat him "all hollow." "Now stay away from this wagon. Don't ever let me catch you stoning my daughter *or* my dog again. Do you understand?"

With that, he tossed the boy down. Tom scrambled to his feet, whimpering, and raced after his friends.

"Idle hands," Kate's father muttered furiously. "Are you all right, Kate?"

She nodded. "He hit my sore shoulder but I'm fine."

He nodded and felt along Buddy's side for injuries. The stone had hit Buddy only a glancing blow but it had cut his skin. "That should heal in a day or two." Then he looked down at Kate. "That was braver than it was wise. They could have really hurt you."

"She's always brave," Tildy told him. "She was the one who smiled at the Indian, making him friendly."

Kate's father stared at Tildy and then at Kate. "What's this about an Indian?"

Tildy told the story swiftly, while Kate shifted her weight nervously from one foot to another. Somehow she knew her papa wasn't going to like that story.

"Then he warned us about the twister and we tried to come home but the cattle herd got in the way," Tildy finished in a note of triumph.

Kate's father knelt and held her by both shoulders. Maybe he didn't know how hard and painful his hands were on her arms as he looked directly into her eyes.

"Now listen to me, Katherine Alexander," he said, his voice heavy with mingled fear and anger. "You are *never* to stray from our sight on this trip. You are *never* to look at, or speak to an Indian. People have died," his voice trailed off, and he pulled her close, holding her very tightly for a moment.

This was loving, but it was such a fierce, frightening loving that Kate couldn't wait for him to release her. Tears came to her eyes. They were not from the pain where he had squeezed her arms but because he was so different. How could it be that she feared him as much as she had loved him in the old days?

The crossing took five days.

The hunters killed several buffaloes and stretched the green hides across the dismantled wagon boxes to make boats. Other men carted hand-hewn oars. These crafts were clumsy but they carried the goods across with the help of ropes and the oars. Then the empty wagons were drawn into the stream at an angle so the current wouldn't hit them broadside.

Kate's father and the Thompson twins half waded and half swam downstream with King and Prince and Duke and Earl. The poor gentle beasts were terrified. Kate finally ran away as far as she could so she couldn't hear them pounding and yelling the huge, pitiful creatures back into line.

During this time, the women dried and smoked the meat from the buffalo into jerky and put it with their other stores.

As if the river hadn't been bad enough, the next few days of travel were horrible. After dragging up a sharp incline, they crossed a broad wasteland, then had to get down a cliff so steep that the wagons had to be held back by ropes. Two of the wagons broke loose and went tumbling down the hill, exploding into splinters of tangled wood and torn canvas.

The women covered their faces with their aprons and wailed helplessly. Kate fought tears of her own. It was as though families had to see their whole lives torn apart to be thrown away at the base of that cruel cliff. Dresses and stew pots and tools were all tumbled together with broken dishes and trunks with their seams burst open, spilling out treasures. A little girl Molly's size clung to her doll, whose china head had been smashed in the fall. A woman pressed a lace-trimmed wedding dress against her chest and wept helplessly. Kate turned away, remembering what her mother had said about few women wanting to make this trip.

"I'd just like to stay here and never go on," Kate decided when they reached the valley below. Giant ash trees shaded grass thick with flowers. The roses made the air smell like home in Ohio. Her mother heated water and washed their clothes. Kate had her first hot bath in almost three months. At night the older people sat around the campfires and gossiped while the young ones danced to fiddle music and played games.

The sky seemed enormous with the moon shrinking toward its last quarter and the sky blinking with stars. If Oregon really *were* like this, maybe it would be worth it after all.

13
Old Bones, New Stones

Kate's worst fears about leaving Ash Hollow were confirmed at once. The sun blazed without mercy. The poor oxens' legs sunk almost knee-deep in burning sands that cracked their hooves, making them limp and stumble. It was too hot inside the wagon to breathe. When Kate went outside, the sand fleas hopped up inside her pantalets and bit her painfully. Mosquitoes surrounded her in a buzzing, stinging cloud. Their bites left welts on her face and arms and made her itch, but they drove little Molly crazy.

Kate's mother, bathing Molly's face with warm water and soda, sighed. "I've tried everything I know of on these stings and they just keep swelling."

"Tildy might have something," Kate suggested. "She learned plant medicine back in Kentucky."

As Molly began to whimper again, her mother dropped her hands in defeat. "Go ask Tildy. If she has anything to ease this child's suffering, I'll be forever grateful."

Kate giggled. "Beholden?" she asked.

Her mother laughed, too. "That's right, beholden. Come to think of it, that's a wonderful word. But wait," she said, rising. "Before you go all that way with those flying varmints, let me hang a veil on your bonnet to protect you from those awful bugs."

Kate reached the Thompson wagon and cried, "Mother sent me to see if you have anything to put on Molly's bug bites. She's swelling up like a poisoned pup."

"You came to the right place. She sure does," Carl said with a proud nod. "She fixed us all up this morning with some witch brew that really keeps the bugs off. Got any more of it, Tildy?"

Tildy was already grubbing back in the wagon. "That was goldenseal," she called up to them. "That keeps them off but doesn't help after you're bitten. Molly needs self-heal. I'll go show her mother how to use it."

"What were you doing back in the wagon?" Kate asked Tildy as they fought their way through the sand to the Alexander wagon.

"Going through our supplies. We're running low on everything. Those boys eat as if they were hollow."

"They probably feel that way. The hunting's really bad in this stretch."

Tildy squeezed in between Kate and her mother on the narrow wagon seat. The distant skyline was laced with the snow-covered tips of mountains. To the south a gigantic rock structure loomed high above the sandy soil. The formation was so big that after traveling twenty-five miles, they still saw it from camp. From there, they saw a second great rock, which looked for all the world like a giant chimney. They camped at a sweet spring near its base.

That night Kate went to bed still hungry because their own stores were running out, too. She lay a long time just thinking about food, crisp fried chicken with biscuits and cream gravy, apple pie with the warm juice dripping off the edge of the pan, and ham sandwiches cut thick with her mother's yeast-raised bread and mustard. She even thought of turnips without a shudder. That had to be a sign of pure starvation.

That night a band of hunters failed to return by nightfall. The grown-ups whispered of Indians. Kate awakened to curious and different sounds mixed in with the morning bugles. She heard the scrape of a shovel and carpentry noises, like sawing and hammering. Once out of the tent, she saw three men digging a few hundred yards from the camp.

"What are they after?" she asked her mother.

Her mother drew in a deep breath before she answered, "It's a grave, Kate. One of the hunters was killed when a buffalo charged him."

At funerals back in Ohio, the mourners had sat in church pews and sung to the deep voice of the organ.

The crowd that gathered by the open grave sang, too, but the wind whipped their words away toward the howling wolves in the distant mountains. Kate's mother clung to her father's arm and wept softly with Molly clinging to her knees.

Kate's face felt hard, as if the cold creeping up from the chilly earth had moved all the way up to her own heart and beyond. The hunter had been younger than her papa, young and strong and married to a red-haired woman with a baby still in arms. Kate fought for breath as the casket was lowered into the earth, let down by ropes the way the wagons were.

Jackson Thompson had made the coffin from the baseboards of the dead man's wagon. When the preacher tossed the first handful of dirt onto the casket and closed his Bible, Kate shut her eyes against a flood of tears and tried not to hear the scrape of shovels covering the casket with sand and loose stones.

As the women surrounded the widow and walked her away, the men began to stagger toward the grave carrying huge stones. Kate gasped and turned to stare at Tildy, who had come to her side. "What are they doing with those stones? Why are they putting a trail marker over his grave?"

Tildy shook her head and bit her lip. "Those haven't been trail markers you've seen. They're graves."

Kate stared at her in horror. "But why? Why do they do that?"

Tildy's voice came rough and pained. "To keep the wolves from digging up the dead and eating them."

Kate felt a wrinkle of dread along her spine. She wanted to scream at Tildy, to make her stop saying things like that, but her words rang true. Kate's head spun, and she suddenly felt a little sick. The back of her throat hurt and her stomach cramped so that she had to lean over and hold it.

"What's wrong?" Tildy asked, taking Kate's arm.

"I'm trying not to throw up," Kate gasped. "I don't want to die. I don't want to be killed by Indians or run down by cattle or buffalo. I don't want to be put down in the ground with my eyes shut and dirt thrown on me. Oh, Tildy, if I die, promise me you won't let wolves eat me," she whispered.

Tildy's eyes were golden on hers. "If you'll do the same for me."

Kate and Tildy didn't talk about the hunter's death again, but Dulcie Hammer did. She did it in a bright-eyed, eager way as if it were nice fresh gossip that one rolled on one's tongue. "That's the *first death*," she said with something like satisfaction in her voice. "Just *wait*, there will be *two more*."

"Do I get to choose who it is?" Tildy asked, staring at Dulcie steadily.

"You are a *disgrace*!" Dulcie said, stamping off.

140

"At least *you* know better than *that*, Kate Alexander."

Kate did know, but it didn't keep her from collapsing into gales of laughter as soon as Dulcie was out of earshot.

In the days that followed, Kate wondered if she would make it all the way to Oregon. She was hungry all the time, and thirsty. The piles of stones seemed closer together as the trail went west. And not only people had died. The bones of animals, oxen and cattle and even horses, were scattered white along the trail. Death was everywhere.

When she brooded about death Kate's mind always went back to her brother. "I intend to live until I see my brother Porter again," she told Tildy in a burst of confidence.

Tildy looked at her a minute, then looked away. Kate knew her friend so well by now. When something hurt Tildy too much, she always turned silly. She did that again. Kate knew in her heart that Tildy wanted to see her "maw" as much as Kate wanted to see Porter, but Tildy would never admit it. Instead, she drew herself up haughtily. "And I," she said, "intend to live to eat ginger cake with cold lemonade one more time."

14
The Thrashing

Kate dreaded the long boring days when nothing happened more than she did the scary times. "I'm sick of miles," she complained to Tildy as they trudged along beside the Alexander wagon.

"You just aren't busy enough," her mother called down. "What would you be doing back in Ohio?"

"Reading, maybe," Kate said thoughtfully. "School would be out so I'd be home. I might be finishing that sampler, or even knitting." She cried after a minute, "If I had wool I could knit and walk."

"There's wool in the back of the wagon," her mother said.

"That's great," Kate cried. "Let's knit, Tildy."

"Knit what?" Tildy asked.

"Socks, maybe. I used to make socks for my brother. The first one is all right but the second one is boring. Don't you think so?"

When Tildy said nothing, Kate glared at her. "*Now* who isn't taking her proper turn at talking?"

"I don't know how to knit," Tildy told her.

Kate nearly jumped with excitement. "That's great! I'll teach you to knit while we walk along."

"Maybe I don't want to learn to knit."

"Of course you do. How else can you get socks and mittens? Surely you don't mean to buy them for all those dozens of brothers of yours."

"There aren't dozens, just a half dozen. Anyway, back in Kentucky folks don't much wear socks except for dressing up."

"Oregon is colder," Kate reminded her.

"All right, all right," Tildy said. "Teach me to knit, if it will make you any happier."

When Kate crawled back down from the wagon with needles and a ball of wool, Tildy bit her lip and stared at them.

"What if I ruin your wool?"

"You can't hurt it," Kate assured her. "We can just pull the stitches out and knit them up again."

Tildy's fingers were awkward at first but by the time the sun signaled midday, she had knitted a thin strip of stitches about five inches long.

Molly was enchanted. "Tildy's making a scarf for Annabelle," she told her mother. "She can wear it when she's cold or when she dresses up."

"We're all going to want to dress up in Fort Laramie," her mother told her.

"That's what everybody says," Tildy replied. "Some women have been wetting their white gloves and turning them in the sun to bleach."

"What a good idea!" Kate's mother cried. "I may try that. Mine are all grimy from gathering buffalo chips."

"We never dressed up for any other place," Kate said. "Isn't Fort Laramie just a fur-trading post?"

Her mother laughed softly. "False pride, I guess. Since it's the biggest post on the whole trail, it's the social center of the west. Some families live there, and that gives it the name of being very civilized and proper for a western post."

"What did you mean by false pride?" Tildy asked.

"They say that settled emigrants look down on late arrivals like us. We all want to look as good as any woman *can* when she's driving a yoke of oxen."

"You always look beautiful," Tildy told her.

Jane Alexander's eyes widened as she stared at Tildy. "What a lovely thing to say, Tildy. You quite startle me."

"My brothers all think so, too," Tildy said. She held her knitting out and stared down at her dress. "Those stuck-up people better not look at me if they're particular. My only other dress is even worse off than this one."

Kate swallowed hard. Why hadn't she figured that out all by herself? Had she really thought that Tildy only wore those two dresses because she wanted to? Aside from the three dresses Kate herself had worn on the trail, she had three new ones in the trunk.

She had never even tried two of them on since her Aunt Agatha fitted them to her.

Kate glanced up to see her mother's dark eyes on hers. Kate had seen that look often enough back in Ohio. It meant, "Watch what you say now." Kate felt insulted. Did her mother think she was going to be rude and tactless about her best friend's clothing? She lifted her chin and looked away.

"I have an idea," Kate's mother said suddenly, in the bright tone she used when she wanted to convince someone of something. "Wouldn't it be fun if you two good friends dressed alike in Fort Laramie?" She went on swiftly to keep them from interrupting. "You both have white bonnets and brown boots. Kate has two dresses just alike in the trunk, one blue and one yellow. If you wore them with white aprons, you would look like sisters."

Kate felt a rush of gratitude toward her mother. "What fun! Amy and I used to play dress-up all the time."

Tildy's face was like a storm cloud.

"I'm a sister," Molly broke in. "I want to dress the same as they do."

Kate laughed. "In my dress? I'm two of you in size. Anyway, little sisters don't dress like big sisters."

When Tildy finally spoke, her tone was sullen. "When you dressed up with this Amy person, whose clothes did you wear?"

"Sometimes hers and sometimes mine," Kate told her. "Mostly hers. Her mother has fancy ideas and goes in for ruffles and things like that. Why do you ask?"

"If you're offering me to wear your dress because you're ashamed of me, don't bother. I can just stay away from you at Fort Laramie."

Kate's mother blushed. "Oh, Tildy, what a thing to say! *All* girls like to dress up. I was trying to think of a way to make Fort Laramie special. It's the closest we'll see to a city on the whole trip. In fact, when we stop for nooning, I'm going to wet down my apron and gloves and pin them to the top of the wagon so the sun will bleach them."

Tildy walked on silently, keeping her eyes on her knitting. "These extra dresses, are they some that Kate's Aunt Agatha made?" she finally asked.

"As a matter of fact, they are," Kate's mother nodded.

"Would you mind taking the blue one?" Tildy asked Kate. The rest of her words came out in a breathless rush as if she had been running. "In my whole life I've never had a stitch of yellow on my body, and it would be pure glory to wear the color of sunshine."

After that it was like waiting for Christmas. The miles dragged even longer, with something to look forward to. Finally the scouts announced that Fort

Laramie was in reach of the next day's travel. That night they camped by a spring. Such a bathing and trimming of beards and hair Kate had never seen.

Kate and Tildy were no exception. That next morning when the oxen topped a ridge, and the snow-capped peak of Laramie Mountain came into view, they were dressed in style. Shouts rose from the travelers in the first platoon of wagons. Some banged on pots in celebration, and a fiddler scraped off a wonderful jig. The good humor lasted through the fording of the Laramie River in midafternoon.

After cautioning them to hang on tight, Carl let Kate and Tildy stand up on the Thompson wagon seat so they could see a grander distance. The white-washed houses inside the adobe walls shone in the late afternoon sun. How lively the place looked, with men and horses gathered in little clusters and women with ruffled bonnets moving along the streets.

"Look at me," Tildy ordered. "Tell me if I'm not all right."

"You look wonderful," Kate assured her.

The confusion around the fort was fascinating. Men speaking a language Kate didn't understand were loading the wagons of a fur trader. Tall Indians in long buffalo robes stood with their brightly dressed wives and scurrying small children.

The walls of the fort were taller than a man, with a slender palisade on top. The huge outer gate of the fort opened onto a small arched passage. The inside gate, which was closed, had a small high window cut into it.

"What's that for?" Kate asked Carl.

"So the guard can inspect a visitor before letting him in," Carl said. "Once that door is open, it's too late."

Kate tightened her arms as she stared at the gate. Even in a fort, there had to be danger!

"There you are," Kate's father said, joining them. "Quite a place, isn't it?"

Kate nodded with delight.

"Your mother is fooling with her bonnet. She and Molly ought to be along any minute."

"Who'll stay with the wagon?" Kate asked.

"We're spelling each other at guarding," her father said. "And nobody's likely to challenge Buddy."

Carl bought both Kate and Tildy immense pieces of apple pie with wedges of sharp yellow cheese. "Never mind that they charged me an arm and a leg," he said, smacking his lips over the last bite. "That was worth a king's ransom in taste."

Kate and Tildy stayed closer than any sisters. They looked and listened and sidestepped strange dogs and men reeking with whiskey until the evening star rose in the deep blue sky. Molly slept on her father's shoulder all the way back to the wagon.

The next day Kate's father and mother bought skimpy supplies at what her father called outrageous prices. The camp rang from the sound of men tightening loose wagon tires, and hammering bent wagon hounds back into place.

Because of the hubbub and confusion, Kate's father kept Buddy tied except for his twice-a-day exercise. Late that next afternoon Kate was helping Tildy load new supplies into the Thompson wagon when she heard Buddy bark. She was down from the wagon and off in a minute. Not only was Buddy's bark louder and deeper than most dogs, but he used it rarely and only with cause. She reached the back of the wagon just as her father came around the other side.

Tom Patterson and his gang of friends were standing at a safe distance and hurling stones at the helpless dog. Buddy was frantic. He barked incessantly and lunged toward them with his teeth bared and his muzzle dripping foam.

Kate's father cursed under his breath, crossed the space in a few swift steps and caught the boy by his jacket. When Tom's coat tore loose, he hit the ground running. Kate's father tripped him, sent him sprawling, then jerked him to his feet.

"I warned you," he said, clapping the boy across his knee and spanking him harder than Kate had ever seen him hit anyone. As soon as the boy began to wail, her father set him free. He hit the ground running again but Kate's father shouted after him, "Next time I set the dog on you!"

When he turned to Kate, he was trembling. "A dog is like a man," he said, his voice harsh. "Beat him enough and drive him too hard and he turns savage."

He closed his eyes for a moment and stood very still. Then he sighed, wiped his hands on his trousers, and tried to smile at Kate. The smile didn't work. His eyes stayed dark with fury. "Let's see what we can do for this fellow of ours," he said quietly.

Buddy whined as Kate ran her hands over his crisp hair, feeling for new injuries. Luckily his old wound had not been split open. She was glad not to have to face her father just then. His words echoed in her mind. Was he thinking of himself when he spoke of men and dogs turning savage under stress?

15
Wagon Fever

The first night on the trail after Laramie, Kate and Tildy were playing by the fire when a stranger approached. Kate had seen the man before, but she didn't know him, or even his name. Something about the way he walked scared her. He must have bothered Tildy, too, because she scooted backward and shot off into the darkness without even a word of good-bye.

Her father set his coffee cup aside and rose. The man was big, taller than Kate's father by a head, and the lines in his face looked mean. "What's this I hear about you beating up on my boy, Alexander?" he asked, glaring down at Kate's father.

At the aggression in his tone, Buddy came to his master's side and rumbled a deep growl. Kate's father silenced the dog with his hand. "I didn't beat up on your boy, Patterson. I gave him a few swats on the tail just as I would my own son for behaving the way he was."

The man watched Buddy with narrowed eyelids.

"That's my boy, not yours, and nobody's raising him up but me. You lay a hand on him again and we settle this as men. I'm warning you, Alexander."

Kate's father studied the man silently for a moment. "Then you better talk to him about torturing helpless beasts. If I catch him picking on my daughter or baiting my dog again, I'll deal him what he's asking for."

Patterson seemed to swell as Kate watched. His hands clenched into fists and his shoulders drew up as if he were ready to strike. From the way his eyes flicked from Buddy to her father's face, Kate just knew that if the dog hadn't been there, he would have struck her father.

He spoke again, his voice deeper and harsher. "Hear me, Alexander. You lay a hand on that boy, and your womenfolk could be crying for you."

Kate heard her mother's startled intake of breath behind her and felt a tightening in her chest.

Both her father and the stranger looked up as Bull Thompson's voice came from the darkness by the wagon. "Let's talk about that a minute, Patterson," Tildy's father said, stepping into the light. He wasn't alone. His sons, all except the twins, who were with the herd, stepped forward with him. They made a wall of men, tall, broad, and silent.

"Alexander's got the right to protect his own. If that means lighting into that little bully of yours, he'll do it."

"Over my dead body," Patterson said.

"That's not the worst idea I've heard, either," Bull said genially. Kate knew it was only hysteria and fear, but she had to tighten her throat and duck her head to keep from giggling.

"That's enough!" Patterson shouted. "You won't always have that dog or an army of white trash to defend you, Alexander. Watch where you walk."

He turned and strode off into the darkness, leaving Kate suddenly weak.

"Well, thank you, I think," Kate's father said, turning to Bull Thompson. "He came here spoiling for a fight."

"He was *born* spoiling for a fight," Tildy's father said. "And his wagon fever doesn't help any. I hope we didn't make it worse for you," he hesitated. "But there's some virtue in knowing where you stand."

"I'm grateful that you just *happened* by," Kate's father said, grinning. "Now that you're here, won't you sit? Jane makes a fair pot of coffee."

Bull shook his head. "It's bedding-down time, but thanks." He grinned. "As to *happening* by, Tildy came flying home with every hair standing on end. She puts a lot of store by you folks."

"We love that child," Kate's mother said softly.

Bull nodded, then turned to Kate's father. "Mind what Patterson said, Dan. He could cool off but I wouldn't chance it. Keep the dog and your gun by you when you leave camp."

That night, Kate heard her parents' voices in low conversation after the fire was out. "We don't need any new trouble," her mother whispered.

"We've come this far," he told her.

"But I'm bone-weary and disheartened," her mother murmured. "And on top of that, I worry. What if the girls get sick? I'm past keeping track of the dangers."

"We're within a week or two of the pass over the mountains," her father replied. "We just need to keep hanging on."

Those two weeks dragged by painfully with the wagon train averaging less than fifteen miles a day. The wind blew constantly, carrying a sharp, painful dust. Kate's eyelids scratched when she blinked, and her clothes worked on her skin like sandpaper. Nothing came easy. Lighting a fire, pitching a tent, even getting food into her mouth before it was gritty with dirt was difficult. The grass was so sparse that the flesh fell away from the oxen, making them weaker by the day. To save them her weight Kate walked in sand that burned her feet through her boots.

When they reached the Sweetwater River, Kate cried with relief. Independence Rock loomed south of them, scratched all over with the names of earlier emigrants. The broad river sparkled in the sun. There was grass for the animals and the Thompson twins brought in game. Kate's mother cooked antelope steaks with thick brown gravy. Simon brought water from an icy pool at the base of Independence Rock and turned it into something like lemonade with sugar and citrus syrup.

Kate ate so much that her stomach hurt and felt like a ripe melon under her hands. She and Tildy sat by the river, paddling their feet in the water.

"This is pure glory," Tildy said, chewing on a piece of soft grass.

"Let's pretend this is Oregon and stay here," Kate suggested.

"We're almost there," Tildy told her.

"Stop that!" Kate snapped. "Papa said this morning that we're running late. We should have been here on the Fourth of July. We may not get there until Thanksgiving."

"You're talking about the Wilamette Valley," Tildy reminded her. "Paw says we're just a week from the pass. Then there's Pacific Springs, where we start going over land that the Queen claims."

Kate stared at her. The word "queen" made her think of Dulcie Hammer. She had barely seen Dulcie at all since she had her brush with poison sumac. But what silly stuff was Tildy coming up with now? "There you go with a whopper!" she told Tildy crossly. "Papa said the land belongs to the man who settles it. How could Mr. Hammer settle land he hasn't even reached yet?"

Tildy exploded with laughter and rolled backward

onto the grass. "Oh, rich!" she cried. "That's rich. I didn't mean the Queen of the World, I mean the *real* queen, Victoria of England."

Kate stared at her coldly. Piece by piece she had figured out that Tildy had no schooling to speak of. The most she could have gone through was the third grade. Tildy only knew what she'd learned from her family and Granny Annie. How would she know who was Queen of England when Kate herself didn't know?

"If you're so smart, just tell me why President Harrison doesn't own this land? It's hooked onto America, and England's across the water."

Tildy stared at her a moment, then swung herself up on her feet. "How can you know so much and so little at the same time? Why do you think we call ourselves emigrants? We're leaving the United States to settle in the Oregon Territory. It doesn't really belong to anyone until American and England settle it between them. Anyway, the President isn't Harrison anymore. He died and the new one is named Tyler."

She stamped away, carrying her boots and trailing her apron across the grass. Kate stared after her. Dumb. Tildy had the same as called her dumb. When Tildy was gone, Kate went to find her mother. Molly was piling stones in her bucket and chattering while her mother finished the washing.

Thoughtfully Kate took the wet petticoat her

mother handed her and twisted the water out onto the ground.

"Who's queen of England?"

Her mother barely glanced at her. "Victoria," she said. "Hold that petticoat up higher. I didn't wash it clean for you to drag in the dirt."

"And who's our President?"

"John Tyler," her mother said. "That ought to be dry enough. Spread it on the grass and start on the aprons."

"Who owns the Oregon Territory?" Kate asked.

Her mother glared at her, lifting a shining black strand of hair from her eyes. "What are we doing, Katherine, playing school? Don't I have enough to do without your pestering me? Both our country and England claim the territory. It still has to be worked out. Now go and play with Tildy or be quiet and help me."

Kate stared at her mother. Katherine. Her mother had not only called her "Katherine" instead of Kate but she had said it in that awful Aunt-Agatha tone of voice.

Kate didn't try to keep the resentment from her voice. "Tildy thinks she's smart."

"She *is* smart," her mother said. "Would you be happier with a dumb friend?" She stared at Kate. "Have you and Tildy had a spat?"

"She the same as called me dumb because I didn't know all that."

Kate's mother stood and pressed her hands to her back right below her waist and made a painful face. She stared off toward the river. "You and Tildy know different things. A girl raised by men is bound to hear more talk of politics than someone like you."

"She's not perfect," Kate said, blinking at sudden tears of jealousy in her eyes.

"I didn't say she was," her mother said, her tone softer. "But she's special. Don't let wagon fever spoil your friendship. She's made this journey bearable for you. And she needs you."

"I don't need *her*," Kate said. "I had friends aplenty back home. I'll have new ones where we stop."

"Not like Tildy," her mother said, leaning to scrub again.

The tears got out of Kate's control, spilling over and pouring down her cheeks. "I hate this trip," she wailed. "You're cross and Papa is mean. And you even like Tildy better than you do me. I wish I was dead!"

The minute the words were out, Kate wanted them back. She shivered at the memory of those piles of rock she had thought were trail markers. Tildy was right. She was not only a coward but a dumb one, too.

In that moment of silence, Molly looked up from her bucket of stones. "Jake told me that probably Mr. Parks is dead."

Kate and her mother both stared at the child. Kate couldn't even remember what Pansy's father looked like, but she could see Pansy in her mind, and most of all, hear her endless chatter, almost as bad as Molly's. But Mr. Parks was a father — like her own. Even Kate's mother seemed to lack words for a moment. Then she asked, "What are you saying?"

Molly shrugged. "Dulcie told Jake that Mr. Parks didn't come in from the hunt last night. She thinks he is the second death."

Kate stared at her. She had thrust Dulcie's terrible prediction out of her mind. Now it came back so vividly that she could see Dulcie's moist eyes glistening too close to her own. "That's the *first* death," she had said. "Just *wait*, there'll be two more."

Kate's mother moved swiftly. She dried her hands, patted her hair, and pulled her bonnet strings tight. "You finish this washing, Kate. I need to call on Emily Parks."

Kate stared after her, then rolled up her sleeves to plunge her arms into the warm soapy water.

"When you get through, can I give Annabelle a bath?" Molly asked.

Kate felt as if her brain had gone numb the way her feet sometimes went to sleep. "Annabelle is made of wood," she said dully. "She'd swell up in water."

"Dead animals swell up," Molly said quietly.

"After a while, they even blow up. I've seen them by the road."

Too much! Kate's mind wailed silently. She bent over the scrub board, her tears streaming over her burning cheeks to drip into the soapy water.

Molly's voice seemed to come from far away. "That soap makes Mama's eyes water, too," Molly said quietly. "Lots of times she stands and spills tears into it just the way you are doing."

16
The Valley of the Bear

Kate's father was in the search group that finally found Mr. Parks's body. When he came home, the skin of his face looked like hard dough. Kate couldn't stand to look at him, but left the wagon to fight her tears alone. What would Pansy and her mother do out here in the wilderness with no man to care for them? They couldn't go back, but how could they go on, just a woman and child alone? She walked along kicking the ground angrily. When she glanced up, she saw Tildy standing by a tree watching her.

For a while, they just looked at each other. Kate felt shy, as if they were strangers who had to start all over again.

Tildy spoke, her words coming out in quick little bursts. "I don't know whether you want to talk to me or not," she finally said.

Kate nodded. "I do," she whispered. "I do. I really do."

"That was rude the way I went off," Tildy said.

"I was rude to get mad because you know more than I," Kate told her.

Tildy's eyes grew wide. "Oh, but I don't. You've taught me almost as much as Granny Annie did. Remember, I couldn't knit or even braid my own hair until we were friends."

"Neither could I play mumblety-peg or know one plant from another," Kate reminded her.

"There," Tildy flashed that brilliant smile. "Now that we're even, can we talk about something else?"

Kate nodded. "Anything in particular?"

"You think of something," Tildy said. "I just had to leave so I wouldn't hear Jackson sawing and hammering."

Kate felt a sudden pain, realizing that Jackson was building another coffin. Kate pictured him, his mouth twisted in concentration as he drove nails with his sure, strong hands. "We could go down to the river," Kate suggested. "We start out early again tomorrow, and I'm going to miss that sweet water."

They were almost to the bank when Tildy grabbed Kate's hand. "Let's go somewhere else."

"Why? What's the matter?" Kate asked. Then she saw Dulcie Hammer and Peggy hurrying toward them through the grass. "They won't hurt us," Kate told Tildy.

Tildy's rough voice came in a growl. "Don't be too sure of that. Come on!"

"Come *help* us, Kate," Dulcie called. *"We're* gathering flowers for *Mrs. Parks and Pansy."*

Kate felt as if she were the rope in a tug-of-war. She was torn between Tildy's tugging hand and Dulcie's urgent voice.

"It's the *least* we can do for *poor* Pansy after what *happened,"* Dulcie went on breathlessly.

"We have to go," Tildy insisted, practically jerking Kate's arm loose.

"That's ridiculous," Dulcie said in a haughty tone. "How would *you* feel if it was *your* father who got bitten by a *rattlesnake* and died and nobody did *anything* nice for you?"

Kate gasped and felt horror shiver down her spine. So that was how Mr. Parks had died. No wonder her father had said nothing.

Tildy trembled with rage. "That's enough, Dulcie Hammer," she shouted furiously. "Go gather your flowers and let Kate alone."

Dulcie stared from Tildy to Kate. "What am *I* doing to *your* precious Kate?" she asked. "If it was *Kate's* father who had been poisoned by a snake and had his body *half eaten* by wolves, *Pansy* would be out here picking flowers for her."

"You *had* to tell her, didn't you?" Tildy said, her voice thick with tears. "I should hit you right in the face. I should stamp on those fancy slippers. I should pull out that buffalo-chip hair of yours."

Tildy struggled to get her hand loose but Kate

held it tightly, fearful that Tildy would fly at Dulcie and fulfill her threats. As Kate gripped Tildy's hand, she fought to control her body. Her stomach had begun to heave. Something sour and ugly had boiled up to burn at the back of her throat.

Dulcie was too busy staring at Tildy to notice. "What did *I* say? What did *I* do?"

Kate glared at her. What did Dulcie Hammer know about a friend trying to protect another friend? "Nobody's fooled by you, Dulcie Hammer," Kate cried. "It's plain as your nose that you get pleasure out of somebody else's pain. Don't pretend you don't know it, either. Tildy knows that thinking about wolves eating people makes me sick."

She barely got the words out before her nausea overwhelmed her. Worse than that, she barely missed vomiting on Dulcie, who sprang back with a cry of alarm. Dulcie danced frantically backward. "That's *not* my fault!" she squealed. "Don't you *dare* go blaming it on me."

"Just go!" Tildy yelled at her.

Dulcie pursed her mouth but didn't find any words. She straightened her back and flipped her head as she walked swiftly away.

Tildy had put her free hand instantly on Kate's forehead. She braced Kate against the jerking of her body as she retched helplessly into the grass.

Kate swallowed desperately, trying to get hold of herself. Tildy went away and came right back with her apron wet with cold river water. When she pressed the wet coolness against Kate's forehead, Kate felt her stomach start to simmer down.

Tildy said nothing while Kate washed her face and hands and pressed the wet cloth against her wrists. Finally Kate tried to smile. "Maybe we should go back," she suggested.

Only then did Tildy speak. Kate looked over at her in astonishment. She expected Tildy to lash out at Dulcie again. Instead, Tildy's gravelly little voice was quiet, almost reverent. "I tell you, Kate Alexander," she said slowly. "I wouldn't have Dulcie Hammer's mean, spiteful heart inside my chest if I was offered the world to take it in."

Kate reached for Tildy's hand and swung it in her own all the way back to camp.

The second funeral was even sadder than the first. Kate stood with her head bowed, unable even to look at Pansy Parks. When it was over and the train started on west, that lonely pile of stones pressed on Kate's mind, bringing tears to her eyes. That could as well have been her own papa. It could as well be her, sitting silent and whitefaced on a wagon seat the way Pansy was, with a stranger riding along beside instead of her father.

After the trail left the river there was neither water nor grass. Both men and animals fought the sand shifting under their feet and the dust stinging their eyes and crusting around their mouths. When they passed Pacific Springs, the nights had turned cold. Kate had to break an inch or more of solid ice to find water in the buckets.

The mountains had been beautiful from afar. They were terrifying at close range with their snowy peaks disappearing into hovering clouds. The oxen strained and panted against their burdens. Even the wagons complained with a frightful creaking and groaning. At last they reached a pass with Bear Valley far below them. The air was so cold that Kate's breath rose in a cloud of steam around her face.

The passage was slow. The river wound through narrow defiles with steep mountains on either side. More than once Kate shut her eyes tightly as the wagons were let down steep cliffs on ropes dangerously weakened by past uses. The animals were exhausted and the men weary and hot-tempered. Her father had become a silent man, rarely speaking to her or Molly and only in terse, cold sentences to their mother.

Inside Kate shivered all the time. She knew this wasn't an ordinary cold that a blazing fire or a thick buffalo robe would cure. Nothing could dispel the cold grief that pressed inside her chest. The real deaths were bad enough, that all those people back there lay in cold earth under the piles of stone, that Mrs. Parks and the red-haired widow stood like ghosts by their campfires. Was it possible that love could die, too, and leave a family cold and silent and uncaring? She saw no love pass between her parents in smiles, or words, or touching. If only Porter were there to reassure her that this would all go away with the mountains and they would be the family they used to be, back in Ohio. But Porter was *not* there, and her parents rose in the morning and went to bed at night, silent and unsmiling.

Her mother had been right. Tildy *had* made the trip possible for her. Tildy was the first person she thought of when she woke in the morning and the last at night. All the *real* fun of the whole journey since Missouri had come with or from Tildy. She had even learned to laugh at Tildy's wildly impossible tales, but only if Tildy would first hold up her fingers crossed so Kate would know what she was getting into. When she was with Tildy, even the shivering was better.

They passed giant blackened craters of old volcanoes. Springs of foaming water surged from the earth. One erupted into a geyser, which sounded like an explosion when it shot upward. Kate, fascinated by the unbelievable things she saw, only half noticed that Tildy grew quieter by the day.

Plodding along beside the wagon, Kate suddenly realized Tildy hadn't said a single word for a good half hour.

"You aren't taking your proper turns at talking

anymore," Kate told Tildy half in fun. "How would you like it if I never said two words to you?"

"I'm sorry," Tildy said.

Kate giggled. "Those were *not* the two words I wanted to hear. What's the matter? Don't you feel good?"

"If you mean by that do I feel sick, the answer is no."

"Is something wrong I don't know about?" Kate asked.

Tildy hesitated, then kicked the earth, sending up a plume of sand. "We're getting close to Fort Hall."

Tildy picked up her pace so that Kate had to run to keep up with her. "Mama says Fort Hall is run by the Hudson Bay Fur Company. She means to buy flour there."

Tildy only mumbled, but Kate was reminded of Fort Laramie. "Remember what fun it was to dress like sisters back in Fort Laramie? And how beautiful you looked with your swinging braid of hair? And the apple pie Carl bought us?"

To Kate's astonishment, Tildy let out a sudden yell as if she were in pain and started running away from the train, bobbing and weaving on the uneven ground.

"Tildy!" Kate shouted, setting off after her.

Kate overtook her at once. She caught her friend by the arm and spun her around. Then she gasped. Streaks of tears had washed waggling clean lines down Tildy's dusty face. Her lips were puckered the same way Kate held her own when she didn't want to cry out loud.

"Tildy, Tildy," Kate said, holding her by her arms. "What's wrong?"

Tildy shook her head helplessly so that the tears ran sideways and began new streaks alongside her ears.

"Fort Hall," she gasped out.

"Why does Fort Hall make you cry?"

Tildy dragged her sleeve across her face, wiping it in one angry motion. "Paw is talking about changing his route at Fort Hall," she sobbed. "Instead of going on to Oregon, he'd take the southern route, going down Raft River and making for California."

As Kate stared at her in disbelief, Tildy began kicking the dirt into a cloud around them. "Men make no sense with their mouths. He keeps scaring himself talking about all that snow and those mountain passes up ahead. He says we're running too late into winter. He's losing cattle already like everyone else. He's decided that he'd be happier in warmer country. He does nothing but talk, talk, talk."

The train was pulling ahead. Kate caught Tildy's arm and urged her to run and catch up. "Maybe Papa can talk him out of it," Kate suggested.

"Nobody in this whole entire world ever talked my Paw nor any of my brothers out of anything," Tildy fumed. "Solid-rock heads, every one of them."

"Oh, you don't mean that," Kate protested.

"Don't I just!" Tildy said. "How do you think Paw got his name Bull?"

"He's big and strong," Kate suggested, panting a little as she kept pace with Tildy's swift, angry steps.

Tildy shook her head and sniffled. "He's called Bull because he's bull*headed*, that's why!"

The significance of Tildy's words hit Kate all at once. California! But the Thompsons couldn't go to California and take Tildy with them. Kate felt her heart drop as tears rushed to her eyes. She couldn't lose Tildy, she couldn't! When Tildy glanced at her, Kate blinked hard, not wanting Tildy to see her crying.

But Tildy *had* seen her tears. She kicked the sand again hard, and spoke up brightly. "I'm amazed you didn't know that."

Kate should have known then what would follow. Every time Kate got downhearted, Tildy went off into one of those wild, silly whoppers to make her laugh and cheer her up.

"Didn't I ever tell you about the time Paw was felling a tree and it came down the wrong way? That big elm tree crashed down spang on the top of Paw's head. Lucky it had been raining and the ground was soft. That tree drove Pa straight into the ground like a nail. It took two teams of horses and the heaviest chain in the county to pull him back out."

Kate had stopped dead-still in horror. "Tildy!" she wailed.

Tildy held up both hands with all her fingers crossed and her thumbs folded over her palms. "I played fair. You didn't even look and on top of that, you spoiled my story. I was going to explain that if that tree had hit him any place but on his head, he would have been killed outright."

Kate suddenly saw the scene as if it had been drawn as a series of pictures in a book, the tree hammering Bull Thompson into the ground like Jackson hammering a nail in wood, and the teams of horses straining to pull him out. She knew her laughter was hysterical from the awful news Tildy had given her, but she laughed anyway, such helpless, breathless laughter that Tildy had to tug *her* along to catch up to the wagon train.

17
Silent Hours

From the moment Kate learned that Bull Thompson didn't intend to settle in Oregon, the cold grief inside her chest became unbearable. Sometimes it exploded in anger. She wanted to scream and strike out at everyone around her. How had her father ever tricked her into seeing all this emigration as a "great adventure"? How was she expected to love and honor a father who was cold and unsmiling and a mother who increasingly spoke to her in as loveless a manner as her Aunt Agatha had? And she couldn't *stand* Molly. Her sister's babbling spun around her head like the buzzing of insects, threatening to drive her crazy.

She seesawed back and forth between this fury and a gray sadness that robbed her life of all pleasure. It didn't matter how hungry she was, her food had no flavor. Even her sleep came troubled with dreams.

Sometimes she dreamed of home, of Porter prancing up the drive on Bridie. Just as she ran to greet him, a mist appeared to block him away. The mist always cleared to reveal only forests and looming mountains instead of the white fences of home.

But even that dream was better than the red and howling dreams of the West. Giant snakes, lumbering bears, armed Indians, and the glittering eyes of wolves brought her whimpering from sleep. Even as she cringed from these terrors, she heard Tildy's laughter fading to an echo through the darkness of giant trees.

Twice in the months since her father and Mr. Patterson "had words," she had overheard her parents whisper of his threats. Once when they spoke of a "near miss," Kate asked Carl Thompson what had happened. He didn't want to talk about it but finally admitted that Patterson had almost shot her father during a hunting expedition. Carl didn't meet her eyes as he added, "Of course, he claimed it to be an accident."

From the beginning, fording rivers had been the scariest and noisiest times for the wagon train. The cattle bellowed their terror at every step, while the men shouted and cursed and the dogs barked frantically. When the raging voice of a swift stream was added to this, the tumult was deafening.

They reached the last ford before Fort Hall. Kate, holding Molly, rode beside her mother for the crossing. Usually she stared straight ahead, unable to bear the sight of the rushing streams with their giant boulders and foaming white water. She never knew what made her glance down. All she really knew at first was that something large had tumbled from the second wagon ahead of theirs.

Only after Tom Patterson hit the water did Kate realize *what* had fallen. The current caught Tom and spun him over and over. With his arms and legs flailing, he was like a spider being propelled helplessly toward the thundering falls downstream.

Kate began to scream. Her father, leading the bellowing oxen, glared up at her, his face twisted with anger. "Stop that, you little idiot!" he called furiously.

"Tom," she shouted to him. No more words would come out. She could only shout "Tom" and point to the boy spinning over and over in the swift water between the stones.

The moment her father looked toward the falls, he jerked his rifle from his shoulder, tossed his hat up into the wagon, and plunged into the water. Kate's mother, fighting the reins of the oxen with Simon alongside, screamed as he dived in. Her face turned deathly white and she began to weep helplessly. Molly, always tuned to her mother's feelings, wailed like a wounded animal. Kate grabbed the child and pressed her face against her chest so she couldn't see the scene in the boiling river.

Kate knew her father was a strong swimmer, but

as he fought the current that threatened to dash him against the stones, she heard herself whimpering, too. Within minutes all the travelers realized what was happening. Wails and cries and shouts of encouragement rose from the other wagons as Kate's father fought his way through the foaming water toward the boy. Kate shut her eyes, unable to bear it, only to open them again and watch her father's frantic course between the giant boulders.

The sweeping current spun in a deadly circle just above the falls. Caught in this vortex, Tom whirled around and around, an unrecognizable darkness against the foaming water, now and then disappearing under the water. When Kate's father was caught by that vicious current, he disappeared for a long, breathless second.

"No!" Kate's mother called in anguish. "No, Dan, no!"

The crowd fell silent as Kate's father surfaced, dragging the limp child by one arm. Head bent against the coursing water, he swam desperately at an angle, trying to tow the boy toward the opposite bank.

Since the Patterson wagon had been one of the first to cross, the boy's father was well up on the bank with his herd. By the time Kate's father neared the shore, Mr. Patterson had heard the commotion and had come to investigate. He ran frantically along the bank of the river toward Kate's father and the boy. This giant man looked possessed by some demon as he leaped and danced among the boulders at the river's edge.

"I can't watch," Kate whispered, without knowing she spoke aloud.

"I can't *see*," Molly wailed. "And I can't breathe, neither."

Kate loosened her grip on Molly as Mr. Patterson leaned over the rushing water, caught his son, and dragged him the last few feet to shore. He tossed the child aside and braced himself to try to catch Dan Alexander and pull him to safety.

He was too late. The current at the crest of the falls caught Kate's father and spun him over and out of sight.

By this time a half dozen men had run crashing along the bank through the heavy brush toward the swirling pool at the bottom of the falls. Kate's mother buried her face in her hands and wept.

The thunder of the water failed to drown out the angry, commanding voices of the men below. Just as Simon led Duke and Earl up onto the opposite bank, a great shout arose from below the falls. Kate's heart seemed to explode inside her chest.

"They have him!" she cried to her mother. "Listen to that. They've got Papa out."

Her mother's dark eyes turned to her with a dull expression. "Pray, Katherine," she said fiercely. "Pray as you have never prayed before."

Kate shoved Molly off her lap. She leaped down from the seat into the shallow water just as the men toiled back up through the woods. Her father was on his feet, but barely. Two men supported him on their shoulders, dragging him through the brush up the incline. His head drooped onto his chest and his arms swung free.

Patterson strode swiftly to his side, pulled him from the arms of his rescuers, and pushed him down on the sandy bank. Kate cried out at the force the man used to thump her father's limp back again and again with his immense strong arms. The end came all of a sudden. Her father coughed, spilled water onto the sand and shook his head giddily from side to side. The cheer that rose along the riverbank sent a flock of crows screaming into the sky. Within minutes he was unsteadily on his feet, and Kate's mother flew into his arms.

Only then did Mr. Patterson turn back to his son who still lay on the bank, sodden and howling. Mr. Patterson jerked Tom to his feet and asked, "Are you hurt?"

When Tom only bawled, his father caught him a sharp cuff across the shoulder. "Answer me then. Are you hurt?"

"I was near drowned," Tom stammered.

The wagon Tom had been riding on was well up on the opposite shore. The owner, the father of one of Tom's friends, strode to Patterson's side. "I told

177

them boys not to act up on that bench but they paid me no mind."

Mr. Patterson stared at the man, then back at his dripping son. Taking a good grip on the boy's arm, he dragged Tom to where Kate's father still stood, fighting for breath. "I'm much beholden, Alexander," he said. "More beholden than any man can pay back. It's a worthless lad who risks the life of a family man. I offer you this. Beat this scallywag any time you get a hankering to. Beat him just for the sport of it, for all I care. You might start now."

Kate's father, trembling with cold from the icy water, and coughing deeply with every breath, managed to grin. "I wager that a thrashing coming from you would do more good. If he feels anything like I do, he needs warming any way he can get it."

Once the Thompson wagon made it across, Tildy came flying to the Alexander wagon. "Paw sent you a message, Mr. Alexander," she called up.

"He did?" Kate's father asked.

She nodded, laughing. "He said you probably didn't do the human race any favor back there, but you got a valuable friend. The worse the enemy, the better the friend."

Kate's father laughed, pulled the buffalo robe closer around his wet clothes, and grinned down at her. "Tell him thanks. It beats a rifle hole in my hat any day."

Kate stared at him, then turned and pulled his

hat from behind the seat. Sure enough, there was a bullet hole near the top of her father's hat. It was big enough to stick her finger through. She began to tremble so violently she had to grip the wagon seat with both hands.

The bright band of cottonwood trees along the stream at Fort Hall rustled and whispered as the wagons drew near. The British flag whipped and pleated itself in a brisk wind. Beyond, visible in the bright, clear air were distant buttes — still more mountains.

Kate's heart ached. Now that her papa had been saved and was even regaining his strength after his ordeal, she had to face the next worst thing in the whole world: losing Tildy.

At Fort Hall there were supplies and hot water, even some vegetables and yeast bread. There was flour for sale brought by John McLoughlin of the Hudson Bay Fur Company. He sold the flour but his lectures to the travelers were free. He warned of terrifying dangers still ahead on the way to Oregon. He spoke of California in glowing terms, trying to persuade the emigrants that the road south was the one to take. Only a few miles west they would reach the Raft River, which would lead them toward this promised land.

While her father repaired the wagon and her mother reveled in clean clothing and boiled potatoes

179

with butter, a rider came into the fort, seeking a doctor. He reported that scarlet fever had struck a nearby mission. He left after taking what medical supplies could be spared.

That night the Thompsons joined the Alexanders by their evening fire.

"We've done a sight of talking amongst us," Bull Thompson said. "That McLoughlin makes the rest of the trail sound mighty treacherous. It sounds like more than you can handle, Dan, with only your womenfolk. The twins are game to stay with you to the end."

"I can't let them do that," Kate's father protested. "Lord knows I need them, but they're your sons."

Bull Thompson stared into the fire embers and shook his head. "I'm not giving you my boys. I'm lending them. We'll get back together again. That's something I believe in strong. When folks want to be together, they find a way."

For a minute Kate didn't dare look at Tildy. Did Tildy believe this, too? Was she waiting for her mother to want to be with her? When Kate did glance at her friend, Tildy was staring down at her blunt little hands and scowling. The little hope that had spun in Kate's chest lay still.

The general wisdom was that from Fort Hall on, small trains of wagons had the best fortune. The first wagons started west the next day. They pulled out in little groups, ten to twenty wagons in a bunch, some bound for California and others for Oregon. The night before the Thompsons were to pull out at dawn, traveling west to the Raft River and on through the great basin toward California, the two families shared supper.

Kate and Tildy sat silently after they had eaten, unable to meet each other's eyes. When Tildy's father rose and declared it was time to "turn in," Tildy got up, too. "Just don't try telling me good-bye," Tildy told Kate in a harsh, unfriendly tone. "I don't like that kind of thing."

"Porter didn't let me tell him good-bye," Kate reminded her. "That hurt me."

"There's all different ways of hurting," Tildy said. "You pick your kind and I'll choose my own."

"I just wish I had something to give you to remember me by," Kate told her.

Tildy shook her head, swinging the shining braid that now nearly reached her waist. "I swear, Kate Alexander, you are the dumbest *smart* person I've ever heard of. Don't you know that if I *need* something to remember you by, it wouldn't work anyway?"

At that she skipped off a few paces, threw both hands in the air and did that crazy little jig she knew made Kate laugh. The firelight glinted on the tears on her cheeks just before she ran off into the darkness.

*   *   *

The next night, with the Alexander wagon already packed to set out, Molly woke up a few hours after midnight. She cried for her mother with a sore throat and a rising fever.

None of them slept any more that night. Kate went several times to fill the basin with fresh cool water. The lantern cast ghostly silhouettes of her mother as she bent over the frantic child, bathing her forehead and throat and arms, trying to stop the terrifying rise of Molly's temperature.

By dawn, Molly no longer looked like herself. Her little face seemed swollen from the raging heat within and her eyes stared at nothing. Her cries no longer resembled a human voice but more the coarse rasping of a wounded bird.

Kate's father moved Kate's things out of the wagon and set up a separate tent for the two of them. "Your mother will tend the child in the wagon, where she'll be off the cold ground."

"But Mother's going to need me," Kate wailed. "I can help her. How can she do it alone with Molly so sick?"

"You can help her a sight more by not getting scarlet fever yourself," he told her, almost gruffly. "And we'll need your help, the twins and I. What kind of a housewife can you be to the three of us?"

Kate stared at him. "You mean, cook?"

He nodded. "And wash up afterwards, and wash clothes, and make butter." His eyes were steady on hers. "The busier you are the less you'll fret."

For the first time in months, he pulled her so close that she could hear his heartbeat through the leather of his jacket. "We're going to get through this, Moppet. We've come this far."

Nobody had called her Moppet since Porter. Her papa had to be thinking about Porter, too, or he never would have used that word. She put her arms around his waist and was startled that they reached all the way, so that her hands met in back. Either he had gotten thinner or her arms had grown longer since they left Ohio. He patted her slowly, the way he patted Buddy, and his hands felt warm.

18
Tears for Tildy

No one ventured near the Alexander wagon through the first few days of Molly's fever. Only Kate's father, who had had scarlet fever as a boy and was presumed safe from the disease, went to the closed flap of the wagon with the food and water and soothing oils offered by the other emigrants.

Kate stood by the tent and watched as her father and mother whispered together. When her mother looked over at her and threw a kiss, Kate forced herself to smile. Tears would have come easier. Her mother's eyes were dark smudges in a hollow face, and her waving hand looked as frail as the claw of a bird.

"How's Molly?" Kate asked. "I wish I could just see her."

He shook her head. "There's little of her to see, and she's too weak to come to the opening."

"Mama looks sick, too," Kate said miserably.

"Tired," he said. "Just tired. She gets small rest and the worry wears her down."

"She needs to eat more," Kate said. "She and Molly both."

"The poor little tyke can scarcely swallow," he reminded her. "Your mother says that rabbit stew you made was the best bite she's had for days."

"Papa," Kate cried. "I want to help more. I *need* to help. I love them both so much."

"And I love you too much to risk your getting that fever," he told her. "If you'll brew up a little cup of tea with a lot of honey, your mother might get it down."

Tea was easy. The loneliness was hard. She missed her mother and Molly as much as she did Tildy. Having no one to talk to, she listened. All the way from Elm Grove, Missouri, Kate had only heard snatches of men's talk, phrases they spoke as she and Tildy passed along the train, and what news her father chose to tell at the campfire. She knew that Dr. Whitman had pushed them steadily on with his words. "Waste no time," he warned them. "Every day will matter toward the end."

Now, against her will, she spent all her time with men, with her father and one or both of the twins. Everything she heard was frightening. A trader at the fort, Richard Grant, warned them that their wagons could not get through the mountain passes to Oregon. In addition, there weren't enough horses at the fort to carry the women and children, let alone the baggage. Others talked of the immense, killing, salt basin that lay on the trail of those emigrants seeking California.

Only Dr. Whitman, who had distributed five horse loads of flour among the destitute emigrants, insisted the wagons could get through. True, the previous attempts had failed (his own and one by Newell's mountain men) but there were enough men this time. The emigrants hired Whitman for four hundred dollars to go ahead with a small party of men to blaze the trail.

Sometimes Kate leaned against the wagon wheel and listened for her mother and Molly inside. Mostly it was silent except for Molly's harsh, painful coughs and a weak, pitiful cry like that of a kitten. Sometimes her mother sang to Molly softly, and Kate said the words along with her while tears squeezed out under her eyelids.

As the fort gradually emptied of wagons, Molly and her mother were offered refuge at Whitman's mission, which already sheltered a number of orphaned children, both white and Indian. Kate's father thanked Dr. Whitman but held fast.

"If we end up being the last one to go and have to go alone, we will. I can't risk setting out until the child's fever breaks."

The Applegate family went ahead as did the Hammer family and most of the others. Among the wagons hanging back was Patterson's.

"Don't delay on my account," Kate's father told

the man. "I want you to take no chances on my account."

"I know when I am beholden," Patterson reminded him.

Molly continued to fight for her life inside the wagon, and Kate's mother grew thinner and paler. Kate's father kept talking about the fever breaking. What if the fever *didn't* break? Molly was so little. Even back in Ohio the old people and the young ones died when scarlet fever struck. Her father's face had changed through Molly's illness. His cheeks were ridged with new, deep lines of worry and dread. Molly *had* to get well. The fever *had* to break.

After supper Kate often sat in the shelter of her father's arm and watched the campfire die. One cold, clear night when the roof of the sky was draped with a scarf of fine, pinpoint-sized stars, he began to talk to her, really talk to her, for the first time since leaving Ohio.

To her astonishment, he began by speaking her brother's name. "I was wrong to vent my fury on Porter," he told her. "I lost control of myself because I was disappointed, just as you were. I wanted my son along and we needed him."

Kate held her breath for a long minute. If he could call Porter his son again, they might one day all be together just as in the old days.

"Porter had as much right to his dream of doctoring as I did to mine of westering. But if I had it

187

to do again . . ." His voice trailed off.

Kate said nothing. Her mother hadn't wanted to go and neither would she have if she had known what a misery it would be. But he had thought of nothing else. What right did he have to change his mind now when Molly was sick unto death and the mountains freezing against winter? They were all there because of him! She wished she could comfort him but it wouldn't be honest. This was *his* great adventure. He'd got what he wanted.

"Three hundred hard miles lie ahead, Kate. Much of this journey I didn't see coming, not the hunger, nor the pain, nor the shadow of death hanging over each of you. This trail has been a grinding wheel, stripping away all that was gentle in each of us. I'm not the man who left Ohio any more than you and your mother are the same. I have guilt for this. If Molly dies — " Again he fell silent.

Kate caught her breath. Over and over since Molly fell ill she had heard Dulcie Hammer's voice in her mind. The peculiar singsong of Dulcie's warning about the "third" death was enough to make her shiver with terror.

"Molly *won't* die," she cried, gripping his arm hard. "You're not *allowed* to think that, and you're not allowed to complain, either. We've come all this way because you wanted to, for your dream."

He turned to her with an astonished expression. "I guess maybe I deserve that. Nobody ever asked you or your mother or your sister if you had dreams, did they?"

She shook her head.

"If they had, what would you have said?"

Kate stared at the embers of the fire, winking scarlet lights in the pale wood ash. "I don't know for sure," she admitted. "Sometimes I've wished I'd stayed safe back in Ohio, but I'm past that now. Maybe dreams change. I miss Tildy with all my heart, the way I used to miss Porter. But I'd go on missing them forever if Molly would just get well."

He rose and pulled her to her feet, hugging her close for a minute. "You ready yourself for the night while I check on our girls. Since Molly can get her bedrest on the trail, we're going to cut out of here the day her fever breaks."

A little later, he returned to the fire with a light step, punched Kate gaily on the shoulder, and called out to the twins.

"It's celebration time," he said, almost shouting. "The fever finally broke. That little tyke is still as spotted as a pup, and can't get a word out from her sore throat, but she's started to sweat and cool down. You know what that means!"

Simon's grand grin split his face all the way across and even Sam ducked his head with pleasure. "Going home!" Simon shouted, grabbing Sam and dancing him around. "Whoopee! Wilamette Valley, here we come!"

Kate felt suddenly weak all over, the way she had felt when the cattle herd swerved instead of running over her and Tildy, the way she had felt when the shout went up from the bottom of the falls that her father had been pulled from the rapids. She didn't have anyone to dance around with, but the excitement was too much to hold inside herself. She backed away and slipped around in back of the wagon. She raised her fists the way Tildy always did and did Tildy's crazy dance, jigging up and down and waving her fists at the sky and wiggling her head as if her neck was broken. Then she stopped a moment, her eyes wide.

That was it! She knew how to celebrate. She had to whisper because if her father heard her, she'd get her mouth washed out with lye soap. But she danced again and pummeled the air with her fists. "Take that, death," she whispered fiercely. "And that and that and that." She called death every awful, ugly, blasphemous word she'd heard from the men in the train all the way from Missouri. Finally she ran out of the really *bad* words. "Scum!" she cried at last. "That's what you are, rotten, lily-livered, egg-sucking scum!"

Then her father was there, staring at her. "What's going on back here?" She knew from his look he had heard the last of her words. Well, let him hear.

She stuck her chin out just a little bit. "I'm celebrating my sister Molly," she told him. "With a song I made up all by myself."

He chuckled and took her arm. "Fair enough, but don't let me catch you teaching it to that little kid!"

She went to bed exhausted. Molly would be fine now, but would she herself ever be happy again in that old careless way? Was that what her father meant by saying she was changed?

Molly was a frail shadow of herself on the seat beside her mother when they took to the trail again. She tired so easily that Kate often took her on her lap and cradled her while she slept. She felt as light as a bird in Kate's arms, and her wrists were so tiny that Kate could close one finger and a thumb around them. Not since she had been a rosy baby in the wooden cradle back home had Kate felt so close to her sister. Kate yearned for the old, happy Molly and her ceaseless words. Instead, Molly stayed silent, following Kate with her eyes and smiling wanly when Kate sang songs to her and made Annabelle dance with her hand.

When they reached the Raft River, where Tildy and her family had taken the trail off toward California, Kate climbed down and walked blindly beside the wagon so that Molly and her mother wouldn't see her streaming tears.

As they toiled toward the next mountains, wolves

191

serenaded them at night. The sound tied Kate's stomach into hard, painful knots. It was cold and the air so dry that the men had to keep caps on their guns. If they didn't, the percussion caps exploded without anyone striking them.

They passed through canyons where huge crickets, two inches long, filled the air, flying in their faces and falling to be mashed to a black, oily mass under the slipping wagon wheels. Finally in mid-September they regained the Snake River. At the Hudson Bay Post known as Fort Walla Walla, they stopped to stare at Wallula Gap, where the broad, sky-bright Columbia burst through the flat-topped cliffs and mesas of lava on its way to the sea.

Kate's father looped his arm around his wife's shoulder and smiled down at her. "Almost there," he whispered. She leaned her head against his shoulder with her face hidden, but Kate saw the weariness in her face. Kate scuffed her boot angrily in the dirt. He was the same as blinded by that dream of his, not to see how many painful miles still lay ahead.

Even as they floated toward Celilo Falls, the men talked of the Dalles, the last great trial they had to face. This narrow rock trough cut between walls twenty feet tall that rose straight toward the distant sky. The river plunged through this gap with a deafening roar. Kate and her mother took turns carrying Molly past the scary remnants of early passages.

Crushed wooden boats and battered barges littered the rocks, visible evidence of the failure of earlier attempts to navigate the treacherous stream. Kate's father and Mr. Patterson hired Indians to carry their goods and the wagons through on barges.

That night by the fire, Kate realized her mother was crying as she held her drowsy Molly in her arms. When Kate caught her father's eyes, he rose and motioned her to follow him off a little way from the camp.

"I had to tell her," he said, almost as an apology. "She's bound to hear the story in time and best have her grief over."

Kate waited tensely for him to go on.

"The Applegate family was not as lucky as we were," he said slowly. "Three died passing this murderous place." He paused and put his hand on her shoulder. "One was an uncle but two were those fine young boys."

Kate cried out. "Not Edward," she said.

He nodded. "Him and the other ten-year-old. Such fine young boys." His voice broke as he turned away.

Kate didn't go back to camp at once. She trembled with a grief beyond tears. Edward *couldn't* be dead, not Edward. How could so much life be over? She pressed her eyes tight, seeing Edward Applegate racing his pony through the spangled grass of Kansas and smiling, always smiling like the first beam of morning. It wasn't right. It wasn't fair.

She hadn't thought much about her Aunt Agatha for a long time. But she could hear the old woman's voice as clearly as if she stood at Kate's side.

"The trail to Oregon is marked by the bones of innocent women and children."

19
A Ring of Bright Stones

The November rain poured in gray, driving sheets when they finally reached the wooden Wilamette Valley. Kate, peering from under the buffalo robe she shared with Molly, stared at the deep, secret forest with mingled fear and wonder. In between the drip and chime of the rain came the ringing sound of axes. But the trip was over. The last mountain had been climbed and the last river forded.

What had she expected to find here? Had she really expected roads and barns and fences with cows staring over at her? Not really, but this valley was nothing but forest, a wilderness of giant trees with now and then a chiming brook winding its way through.

One great evergreen tree looked very like the next one to Kate. She marveled that her father seemed to know where he was going. He followed streams and chose one primitive trail over another, as if the endless trees themselves were talking to him. Sometimes he stopped at a clearing. Usually he didn't even dismount, but rode Chessie to where the men were working, spoke with them briefly, and returned.

"Is he going to stop and talk to every settler in Oregon?" Kate asked her mother crossly, tired of being bumped along in the wagon.

Her mother's dark eyes turned to her. "What a little grump you are! Try smiling."

"I'm wet and cold and have nothing to smile about."

To her astonishment, her mother laughed almost merrily. Kate looked at her suspiciously. "Why are *you* so happy?" she asked, not even caring that she sounded sullen.

"Because we're almost home, at last," her mother said quietly. Then she fairly twinkled and added, "And Papa and I have a grand surprise for you."

For three nights they camped in the forest. Owls called plaintively, then flew away, their wings whispering in the darkness. Strange birds called, twigs snapped, and some animal crept furtively through the rustling fallen leaves. Yellow eyes shone back at Kate from the brush and Buddy trembled and whined under her arm. After that she didn't look out at night.

Finally her father stopped, slid from Chessie's back and came around to lift his wife down. He kissed her soundly on both cheeks. "We're here," he said. "This is it. Home."

Kate stared at the huge trees towering around them. It looked like every other bit of the forest to her. "How do you know this is the right place?" Kate asked.

He grinned at her and thumped her shoulder. "I was given directions. Did your mother tell you we had a surprise for you?"

"Now?" she asked.

"Later," he told her. "Don't you want to see your new home?"

He was so happy and proud that she swallowed her disappointment. How could anyone feel at home in this strange, desolate place? And how dark it was, even in midday. She had to look straight up to see the sun gilding the needles of the tops of the trees.

"Come along," he ordered, talking. He was as jabbery as Molly. He would walk and stop, then spread out his hands. "The road will go here." He ran a few steps up a small incline. "See this higher ground along here? The cabin will sit right on this knoll. We'll start with a single room and build on." He led her to where he planned to set the barn and where he would clear a field to grow hay for the stock.

If it hadn't been so strange, it would have been funny. How could he look at this forest and see a whole farm? "Of course, the trees will have to come out," Kate said, not even trying to hide her grin.

"I see it, Kate," he said. "I see it as plain as if it were all finished and the four of us happy together like the old days."

She *made* herself imagine it: the field, the barn, and the log house complete with smoke trailing from its stone chimney.

"Will we have neighbors?" she asked.

Her father nodded. "The Pattersons are claiming not far from here. We'll even have next-door neighbors before it's done. This is the best of the land and the richest of the soil. Did I mention our orchard? We'll grow such apples here as would pass for pumpkins back in Ohio."

She was about to ask about school and church when he led her through the woods to the bank of a small, swift creek. "I saved the best for the last," he said. "Did you ever hear such a sweet-voiced stream?"

Buddy had galloped ahead to plunge ankle-deep in the water. Bright fish darted away from him in clear water that sang as it passed over the stones. "How did you know about this place?" she asked, beginning to get excited in spite of herself.

"Good directions," he said. "We're among the last of the train to get here, you know. Our friends looked out for us and left word."

"Is it time for the surprise yet?" she asked as they walked back to the wagon.

He shook his head. "It will come when it comes."

"What kind of a surprise is it?" she asked.

"That," he said with a wink, "is for me to know and you to wonder about."

Kate glared at him but said nothing. Suddenly he and her mother were just alike, unaccountably happy for no sensible reason. He was dreaming of the house and the barn and the orchard in the shade of these endless trees. They still had no roof over their heads, and the rain kept falling with just little spurts of sunshine coming in between the showers.

The first couple of days Kate and her mother did nothing but wash clothes and cook for her father and the twins. All day they swung their axes, felling trees where the house would stand. By the third day the noise was almost more than Kate could stand. Her mother didn't seem to notice. She had sheltered her cook fire with a tent of canvas and was stirring something in a bowl. Kate couldn't remember the last time she had heard her mother singing softly to herself as she worked.

"Molly and I want to go off somewhere to play," Kate said. "We could make a playhouse by the stream."

"Don't go any farther than that," her mother cautioned. "And stay well back from the water lest Molly fall in."

Kate held Molly's hand as they stared at the tumbling brook. "We'll build our own house here," she said. "For us and Annabelle."

Molly, who had suffered with her swollen throat, only nodded agreement. Kate's back had begun to hurt a little from the weight of the stones by the time she had outlined a good-sized square room.

"This is the door," she told Molly, pointing to the opening she had left. "You mustn't ever step over the wall but must come in through the door."

Molly grinned and held her skirt flat against her sides as she walked in.

"How do you do!" Kate told her in a bright voice. "How nice of you to come. Do sit down and I'll brew tea."

As Molly sat primly on a stone with her hands on her lap, she suddenly whispered, "The axes stopped."

"You're right," Kate agreed, pausing to listen. "Papa probably has company."

Kate reached for the make-believe teapot, which was really only a round stone and nodded. "Your tea will be ready any minute now." If it was only men to see her father, she wasn't really interested.

"We have company, too," Molly whispered very quietly.

Something about Molly's tone was scary. Maybe it was a bear or even a panther. Kate caught a deep breath and turned to look down the path. She stared hard a moment, then felt her heart begin to thunder. She shut her eyes a moment, then looked again. This had to be a waking dream. Tildy, with her bonnet strings hanging and new smudges on that same old dress, was running down the path toward them. Her golden eyes glistened and the gap shone in the front of her smile.

"Surprise!" she shouted in that wonderful scratchy voice. "Surprise! Surprise! Surprise!"

Kate could not have moved or spoken for her life, but Molly wasn't even disturbed. "Come in through the door," Molly called. "Don't step through the wall."

Tildy paid no attention but leaped the row of stones and grabbed Kate hard around the middle, dancing her about. "Isn't this glory?" she asked Kate.

Kate clung to her with tears streaming. She tried to pick Tildy up to swing her around but couldn't get her off the ground. "I thought you were gone," she cried. "Clear off in California."

Tildy grinned her gap-toothed smile. "We did start, but Paw got his dander up and came back. Can you believe that we put our claim on the very next section to you? I wanted to come right over when you pulled in, but Paw and the boys were raising the roof and it needed doing." Tildy glanced at Molly and asked very seriously. "Which one of these chairs is mine?"

As Molly patted the stone beside her, Kate heard her father calling. Kate had a million questions, but didn't get to ask any of them. Tildy chattered steadily all the way to the clearing.

"There she is," Bull Thompson called as Kate approached. He swung her off her feet and kissed her roundly, before handing her on to Titus, who passed her on to Jackson and the rest of the brothers as if she were the ball in a game of keep-away.

Then he reached for Molly, set her on his shoulders, and plopped his hat over her bonnet. "That's better!" he said with satisfaction.

Kate's father grinned at her. "How's that for a surprise?" he asked. She grabbed him tight around the waist, there not being words enough.

"Come sit down," Kate's mother called. "The gingerbread is done."

"I smell it," Tildy said. "I've been smelling for gingerbread all the way from Kentucky."

"That girl and her whoppers," Carl said, shaking his head.

Kate finally got her chance. "Mr. Thompson," she cried. "I'm so happy I could pop, but what happened to your going to California?"

Bull Thompson scowled. "I'm a man who makes up his own mind. I had full decided to go south when I started thinking about that John McLoughlin."

His voice rose angrily as he turned to Kate's father. "Dan, did you hear him trying to keep us all from coming to Oregon? He got my dander up. No man is going to tell Bull Thompson where to settle! We just plain turned around and came back up here where we started out for from the first." He grinned at Kate. "Believe me, things got more comfortable with that Tildy tyke the minute we headed north."

Kate turned to see Tildy's eyes full and golden and laughing on her own. Kate fought to keep from laughing out loud as she heard Tildy's whopper again in her mind. She leaned close to Tildy and whispered softly, "If that tree had hit him any place but on his head he would have been killed outright."

Suddenly they were both laughing so helplessly that they had to hold each other up. Kate's mother banged on her pot with a wooden spoon. "Straighten up, you little scamps! Come and eat this gingerbread before I throw it out."

Molly sat on a piece of canvas between Kate and Tildy. With the first bite of the gingerbread and sip of warm tea, Molly began to talk. Kate and Tildy stared at her. Molly didn't even stop chattering when she took bites. The words poured out of her mouth the way the herds of antelope had streamed over the prairie grasses and the rushing rivers charged through the mountain passes.

Kate giggled softly. "I can't believe I ever said I couldn't wait to hear that child start talking again."

Tildy shrugged and licked the last crumb from her fingers. "We'll have time to take turns," she whispered. "Lots of time."

As Kate smiled at her, the wind rose, stirring the tops of the giant trees. She heard the voice of the brook splashing over its stones and the cry of a strange bird somewhere in the distance. The little shivering that had never completely gone away stirred again along her spine. This was all so strange and much of it was scary. But her mother and father were standing close together and laughing at something that Simon had said to his father. The clearing smelled of pine pitch, and wood smoke, and gingerbread, and Tildy was going to live next door.

Maybe settling in would be a grand adventure. And this time the dream was partly hers, too.